MINECRAFT™
OPEN WORLD

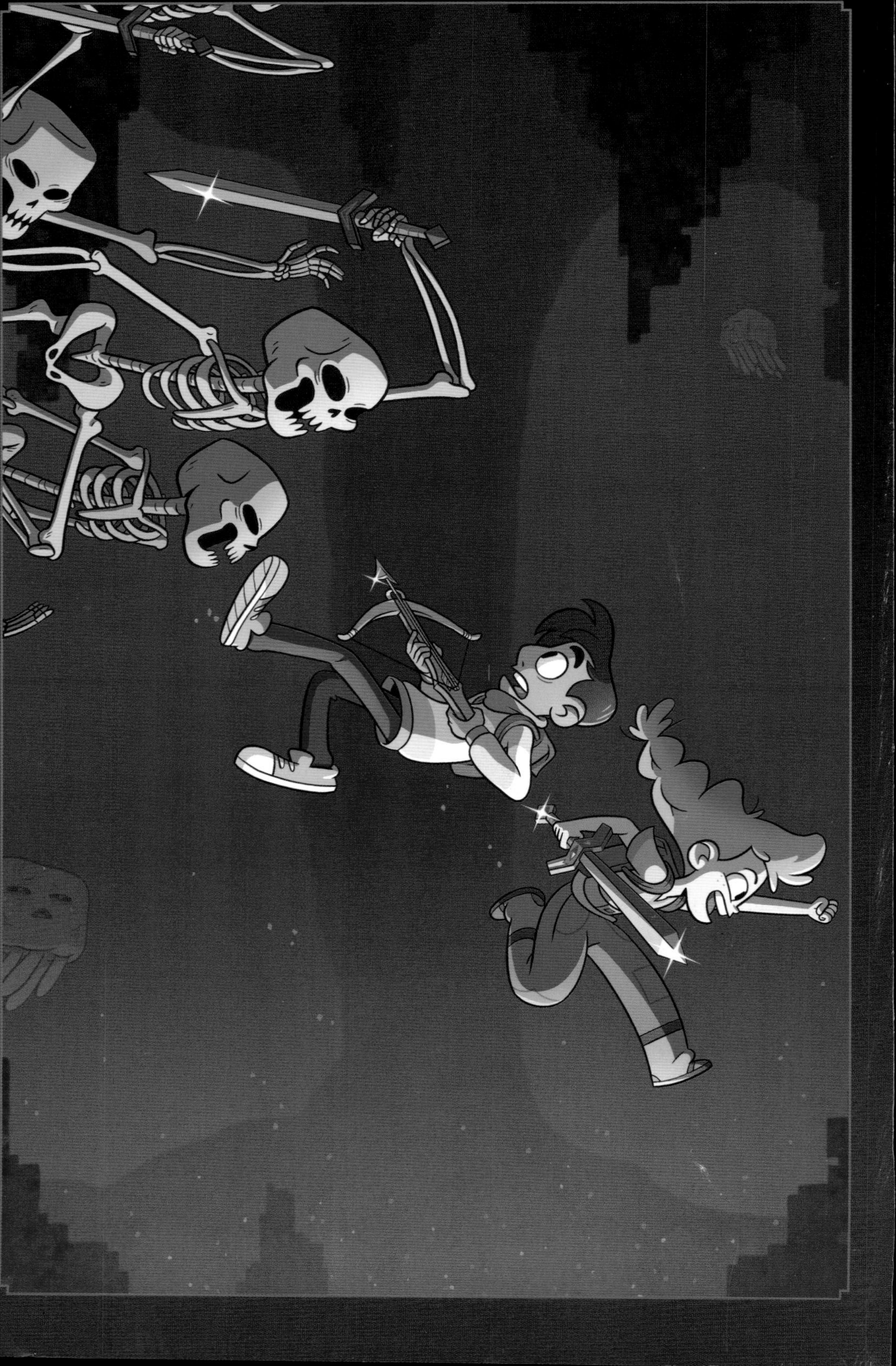

MINECRAFT
OPEN WORLD

INTO THE NETHER

BY
STEPHANIE RAMIREZ

LETTERED BY
RACHELLE REYES

DARK HORSE BOOKS

PRESIDENT & PUBLISHER
MIKE RICHARDSON

EDITOR
SHANTEL LaROCQUE

ASSOCIATE EDITOR
BRETT ISRAEL

ASSISTANT EDITOR
SANJAY DHARAWAT

DESIGNER
KEITH WOOD

DIGITAL ART TECHNICIAN
SAMANTHA HUMMER

SPECIAL THANKS TO
**ALEX WILTSHIRE,
KELSEY HOWARD,** AND
SHERIN KWAN

Published by Dark Horse Books
A division of Dark Horse Comics LLC
10956 SE Main Street
Milwaukie, OR 97222

MINECRAFT.NET
DARKHORSE.COM

To find a comics shop in your area, visit ComicShopLocator.com.

First edition: November 2022
Ebook ISBN 978-1-50671-891-0
Trade paperback ISBN 978-1-50671-888-0

10 9 8 7 6 5 4 3 2 1

Printed in China

NEIL HANKERSON
Executive Vice President

TOM WEDDLE
Chief Financial Officer

DALE LAFOUNTAIN
Chief Information Officer

TIM WIESCH
Vice President of Licensing

VANESSA TODD-HOLMES
Vice President of Production and Scheduling

MARK BERNARDI
Vice President of Book Trade and Digital Sales

RANDY LAHRMAN
Vice President of Product Development and Sales

KEN LIZZI
General Counsel

DAVE MARSHALL
Editor in Chief

DAVEY ESTRADA
Editorial Director

CHRIS WARNER
Senior Books Editor

CARA O'NEIL
Senior Director of Marketing

CARY GRAZZINI
Director of Specialty Projects

LIA RIBACCHI
Art Director

MICHAEL GOMBOS
Senior Director of Licensed Publications

KARI YADRO
Director of Custom Programs

KARI TORSON
Director of International Licensing

CHRISTINA NIECE
Director of Scheduling

MIX
Paper from responsible sources
FSC
www.fsc.org   FSC® C109093

Library of Congress Cataloging-in-Publication Data

Names: Ramirez, Stephanie, writer, illustrator. | Reyes, Rachelle, letterer.
Title: Minecraft: open world - into the nether / written and illustrated by Stephanie Ramirez ; lettered by Rachelle Reyes.
Description: First edition. | Milwaukie, OR : Dark Horse Books, 2022. | "Mojang Studios" | Summary: Sarah is new to the world of Minecraft, so she turns to veteran player Hector for help, but after showing reluctance, Sarah's enthusiasm and all-around energy bring Hector around, and the two become partners and friends.
Identifiers: LCCN 2022024155 (print) | LCCN 2022024156 (ebook) | ISBN 9781506718880 (trade paperback) | ISBN 9781506718910 (ebook)
Subjects: CYAC: Graphic novels. | Minecraft (Game)--Fiction. | Video games--Fiction. | Friendship--Fiction. | LCGFT: Action and adventure comics. | Graphic novels.
Classification: LCC PZ7.7.R486 Min 2022 (print) | LCC PZ7.7.R486 (ebook) | DDC 741.5/973--dc23/eng/20220525
LC record available at https://lccn.loc.gov/2022024155
LC ebook record available at https://lccn.loc.gov/2022024156

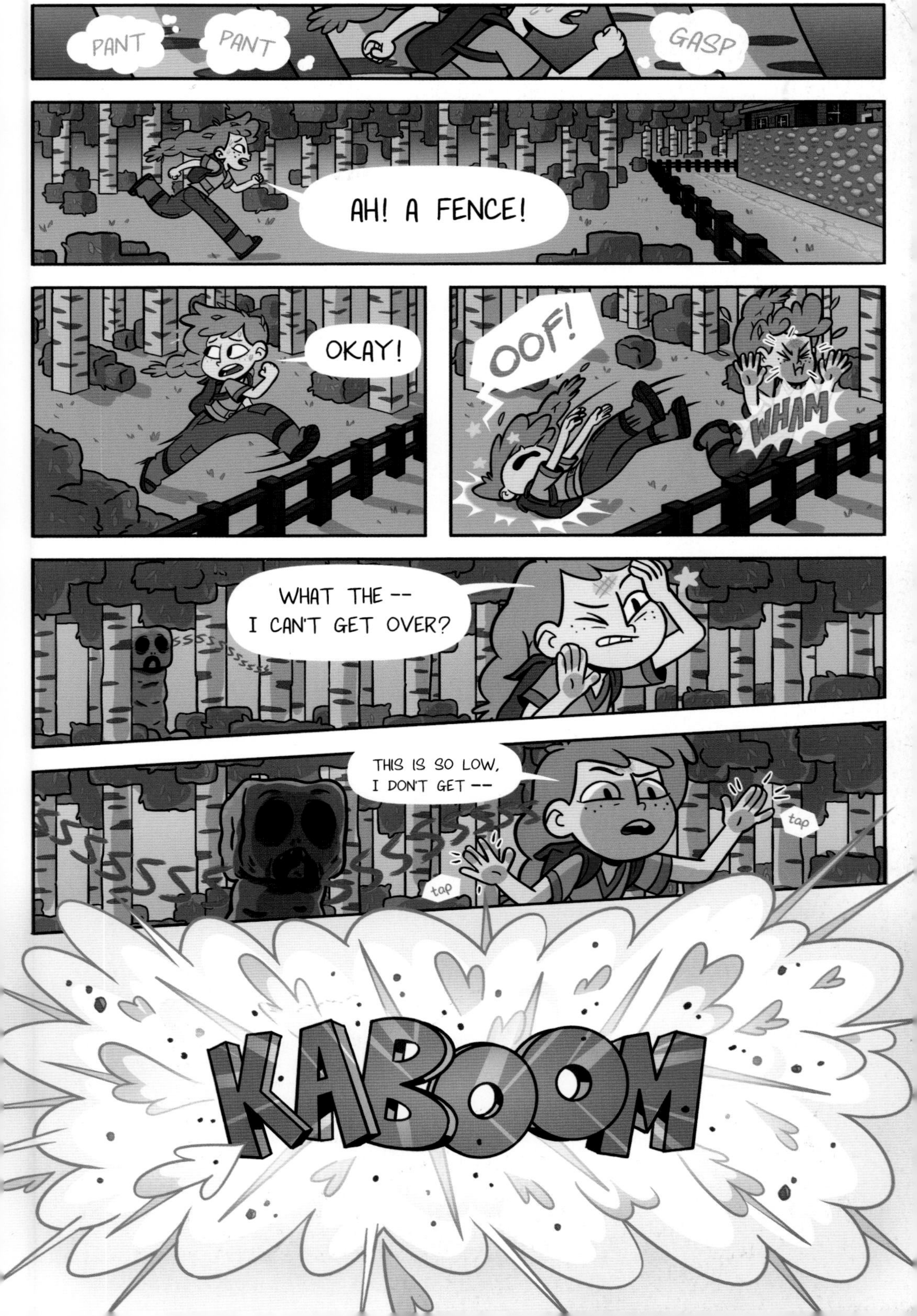
PANT
PANT
GASP
AH! A FENCE!
OKAY!
OOF!
WHAM
WHAT THE --
I CAN'T GET OVER?
sssssssssss
THIS IS SO LOW,
I DON'T GET --
tap
tap
KABOOM

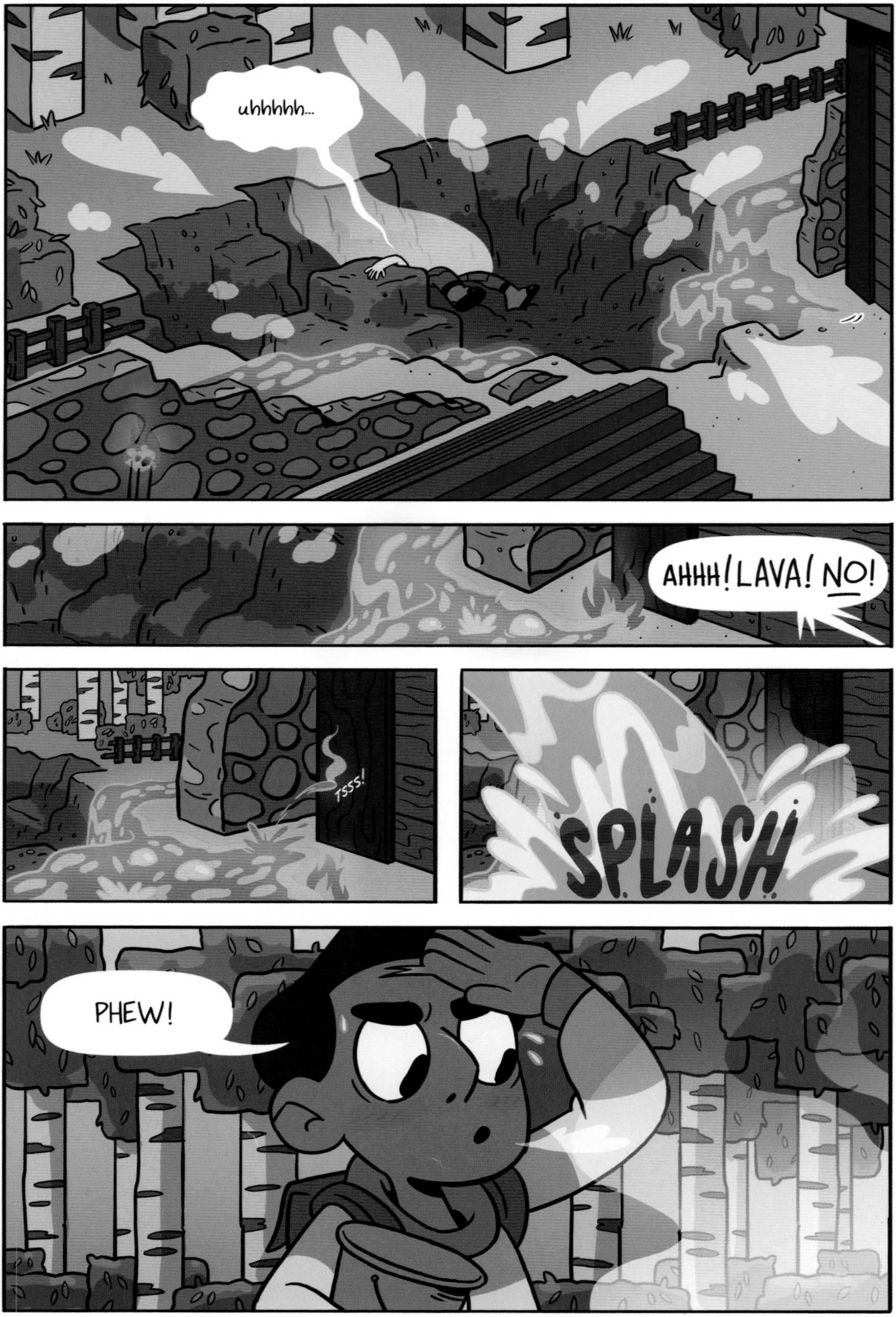
uhhhhh...
AHHH! LAVA! NO!
TSSS!
SPLASH
PHEW!

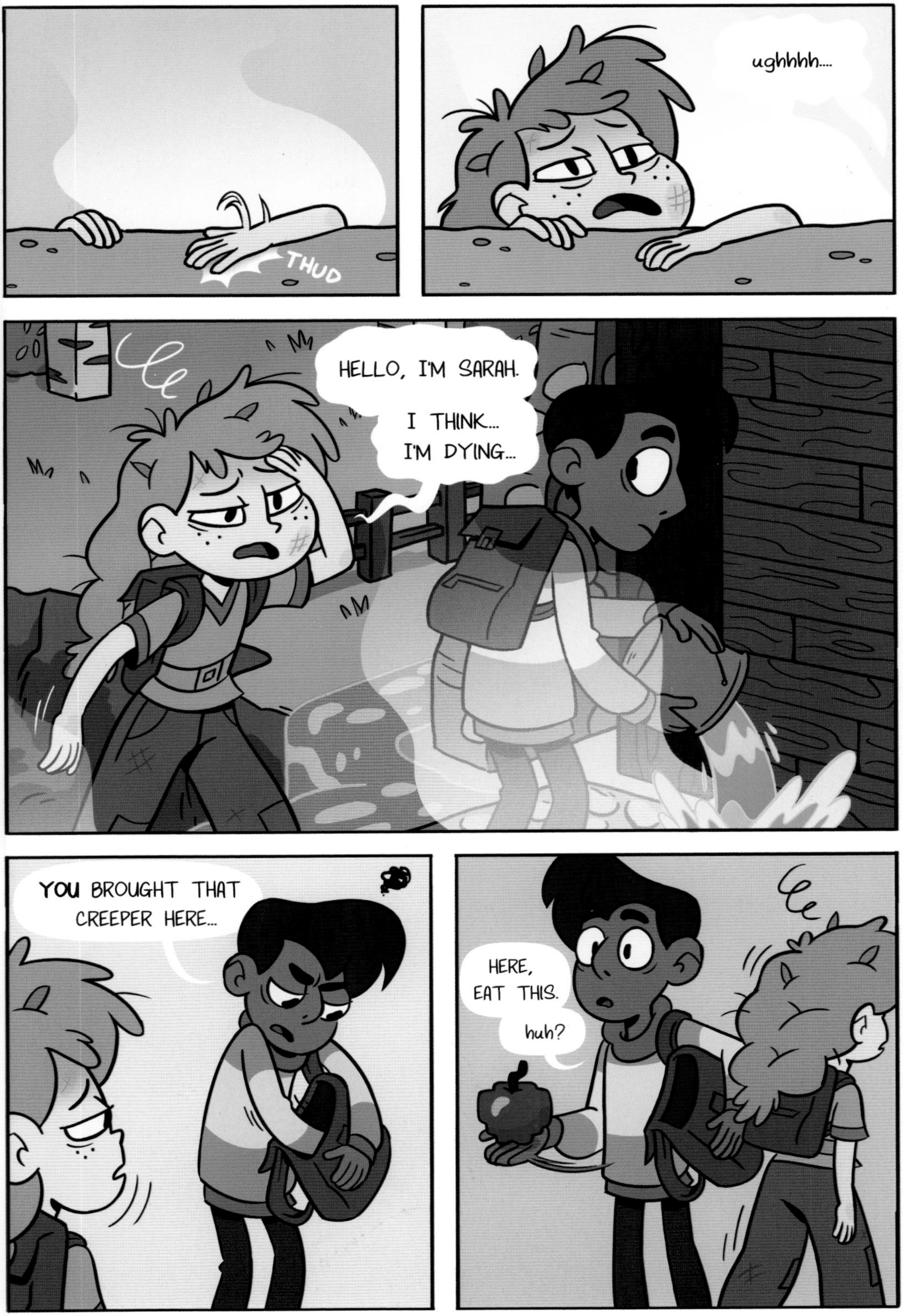
THUD
ughhhh....
HELLO, I'M SARAH.
I THINK... I'M DYING...
YOU BROUGHT THAT CREEPER HERE...
HERE, EAT THIS.
huh?

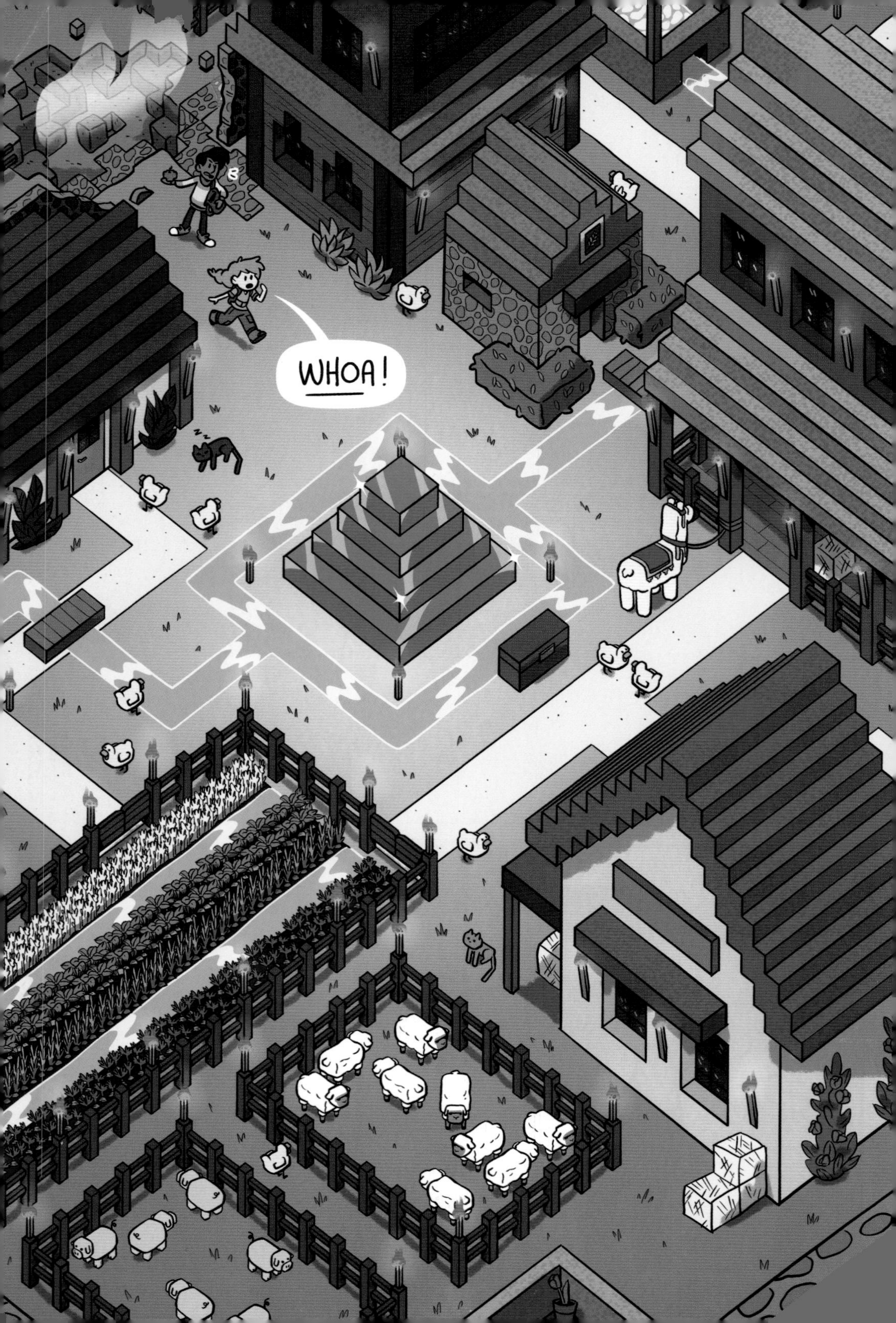

WHOA!

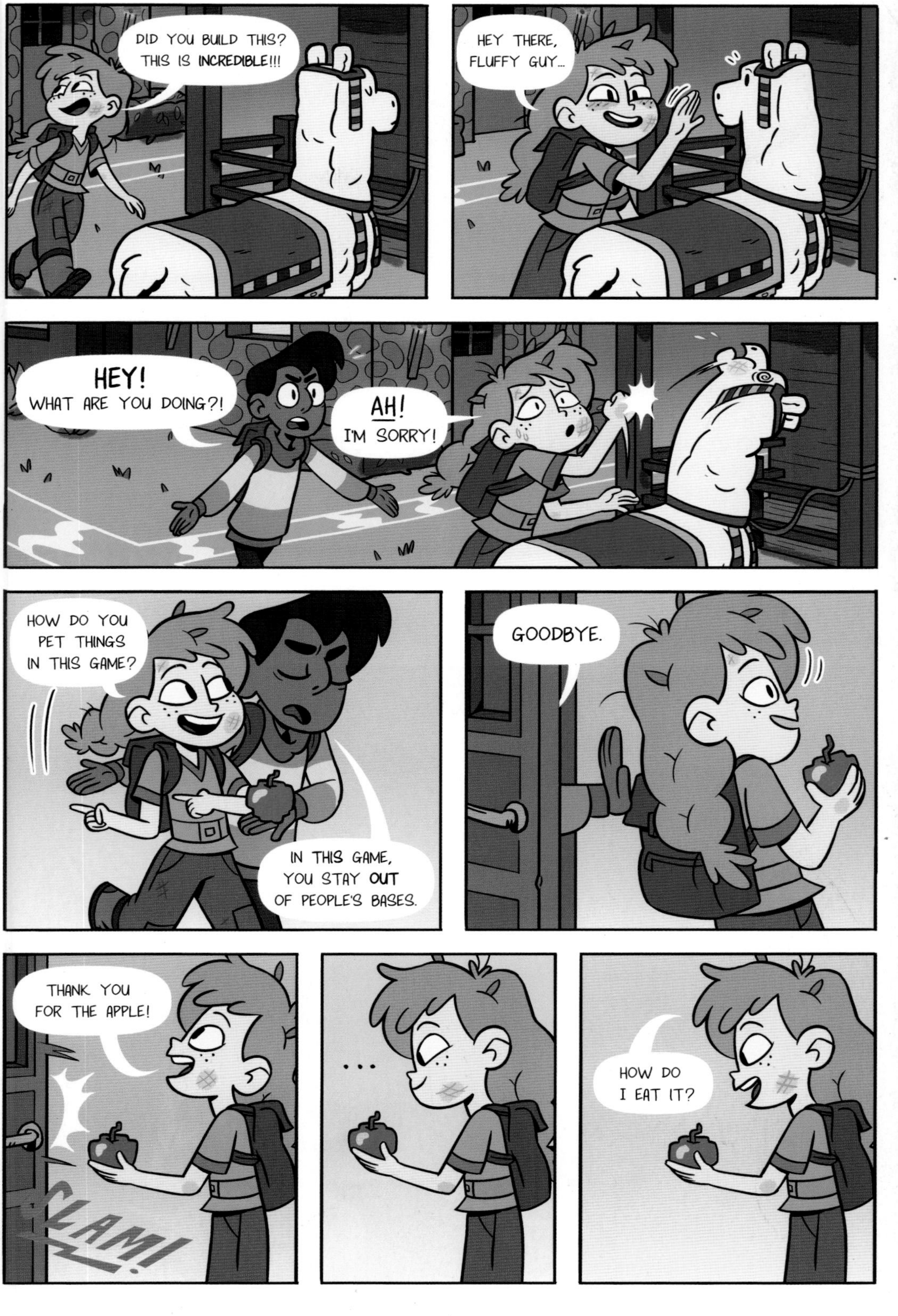
DID YOU BUILD THIS? THIS IS INCREDIBLE!!!
HEY THERE, FLUFFY GUY...
HEY! WHAT ARE YOU DOING?!
AH! I'M SORRY!
HOW DO YOU PET THINGS IN THIS GAME?
IN THIS GAME, YOU STAY OUT OF PEOPLE'S BASES.
GOODBYE.
THANK YOU FOR THE APPLE!
SLAM!
...
HOW DO I EAT IT?

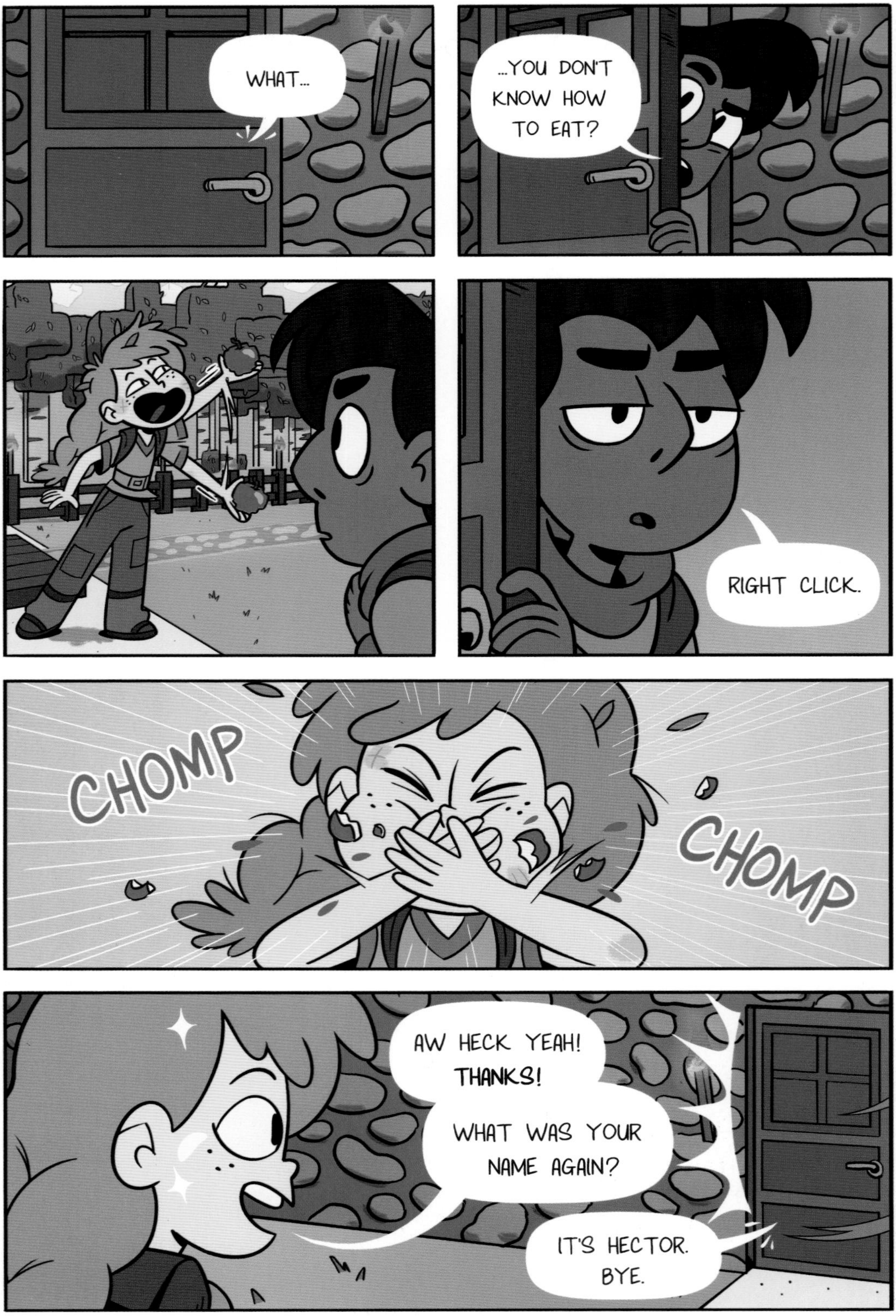
WHAT...
...YOU DON'T KNOW HOW TO EAT?
RIGHT CLICK.
CHOMP
CHOMP
AW HECK YEAH! THANKS!
WHAT WAS YOUR NAME AGAIN?
IT'S HECTOR. BYE.

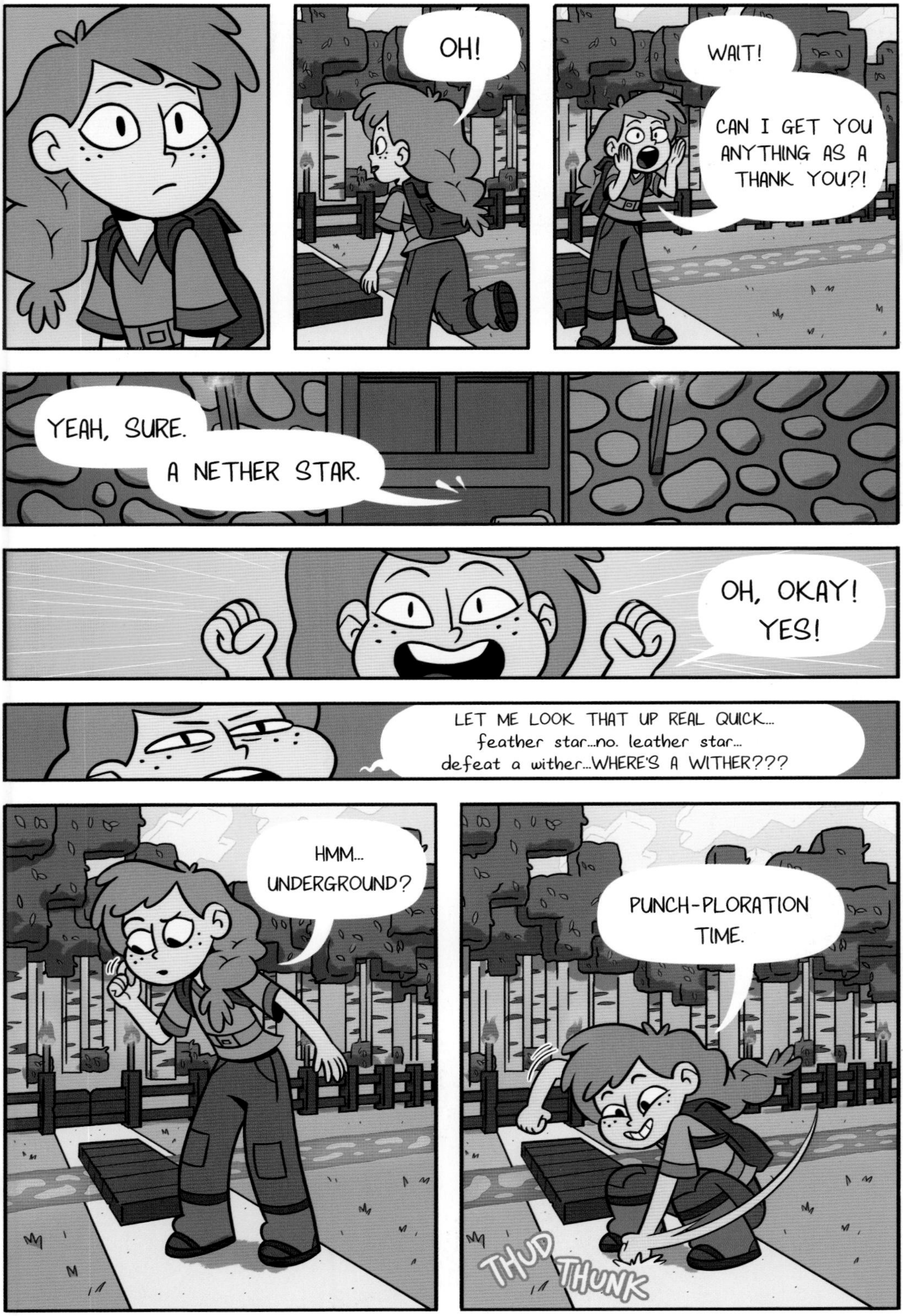
OH!
WAIT!
CAN I GET YOU ANYTHING AS A THANK YOU?!
YEAH, SURE.
A NETHER STAR.
OH, OKAY! YES!
LET ME LOOK THAT UP REAL QUICK... feather star...no. leather star... defeat a wither...WHERE'S A WITHER???
HMM... UNDERGROUND?
PUNCH-PLORATION TIME.
THUD
THUNK

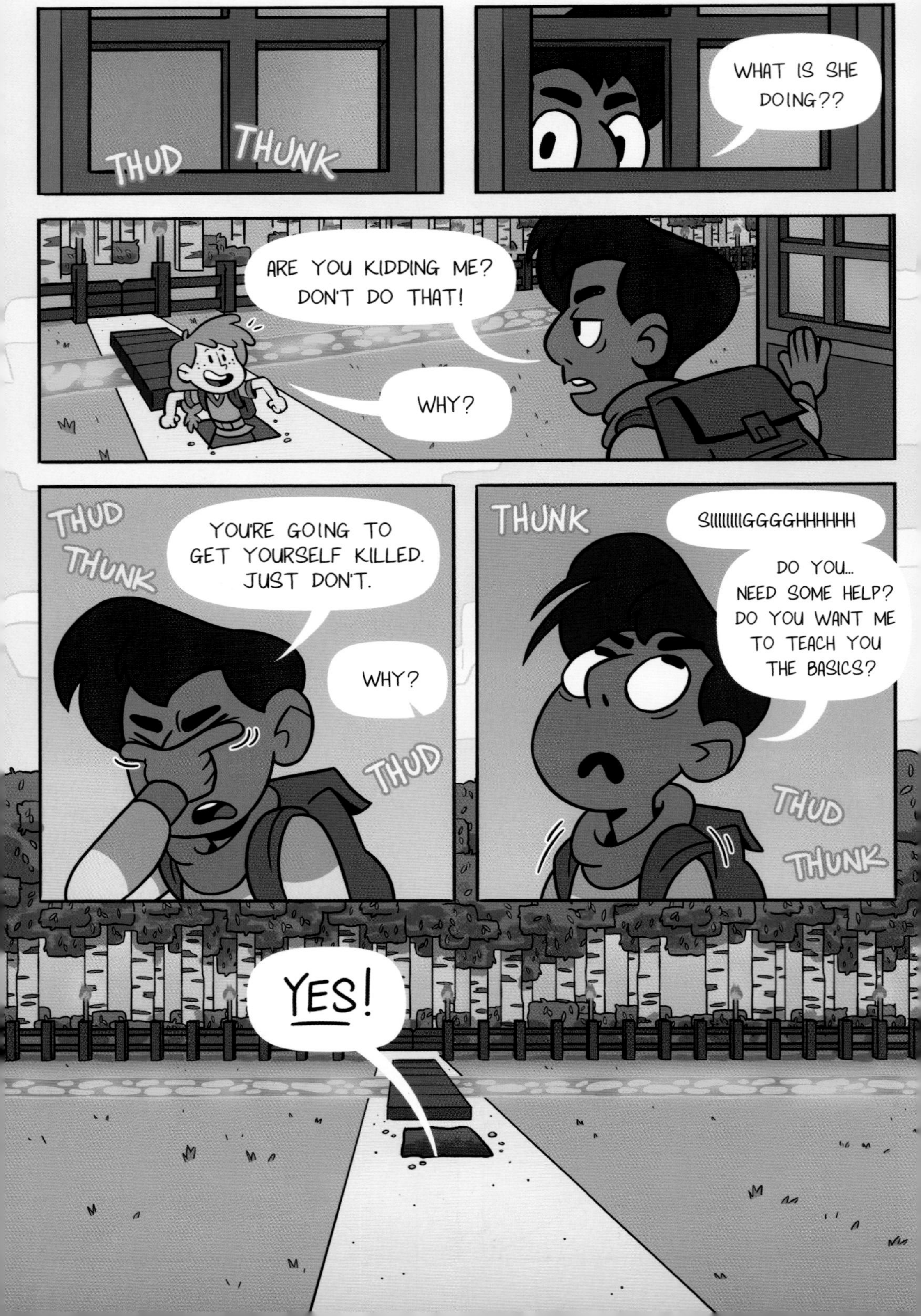
THUD
THUNK
WHAT IS SHE DOING??
ARE YOU KIDDING ME? DON'T DO THAT!
WHY?
THUD
THUNK
YOU'RE GOING TO GET YOURSELF KILLED. JUST DON'T.
WHY?
THUD
THUNK
SIIIIIIIGGGGHHHHHH
DO YOU... NEED SOME HELP? DO YOU WANT ME TO TEACH YOU THE BASICS?
THUD
THUNK
YES!

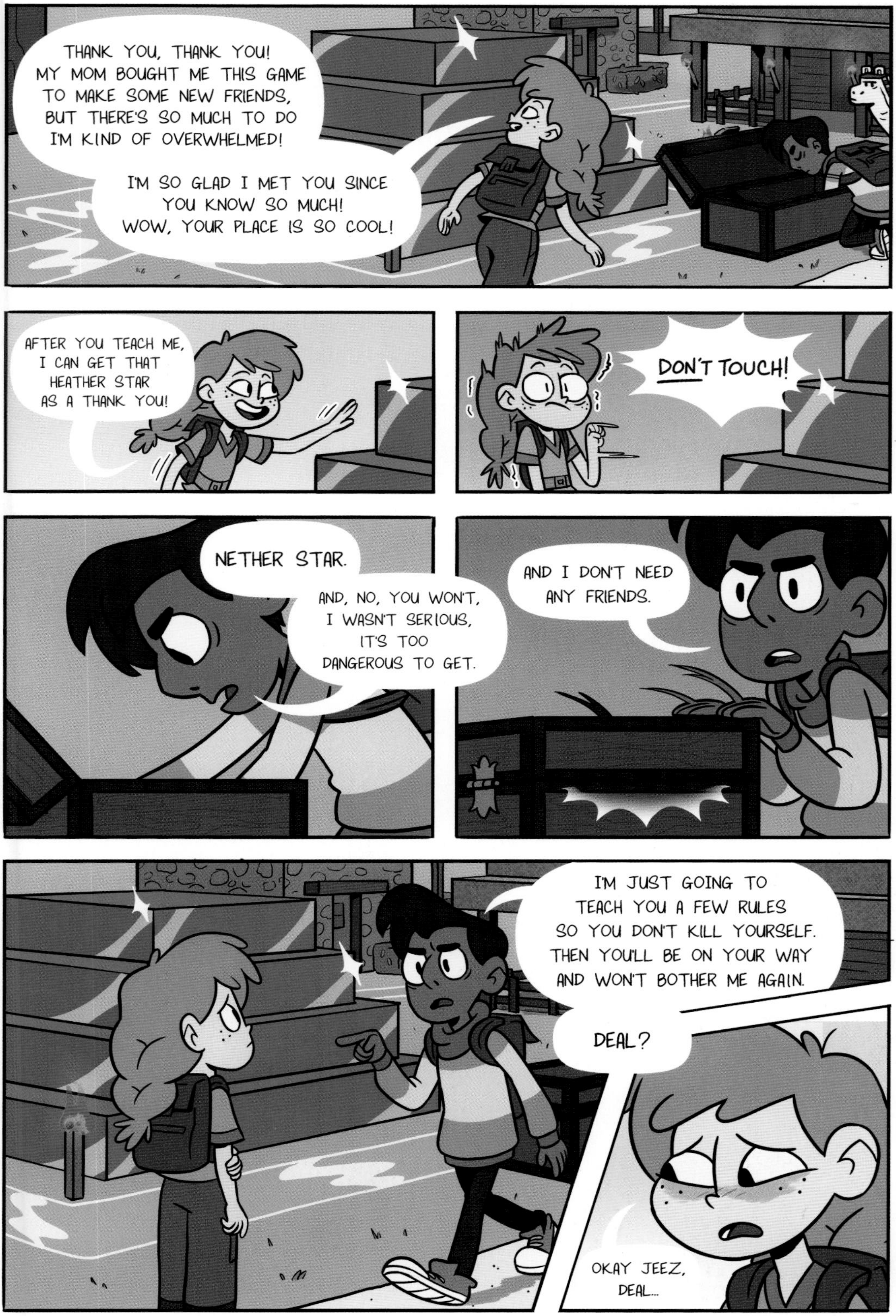
THANK YOU, THANK YOU! MY MOM BOUGHT ME THIS GAME TO MAKE SOME NEW FRIENDS, BUT THERE'S SO MUCH TO DO I'M KIND OF OVERWHELMED!
I'M SO GLAD I MET YOU SINCE YOU KNOW SO MUCH! WOW, YOUR PLACE IS SO COOL!
AFTER YOU TEACH ME, I CAN GET THAT HEATHER STAR AS A THANK YOU!
DON'T TOUCH!
NETHER STAR.
AND, NO, YOU WON'T, I WASN'T SERIOUS, IT'S TOO DANGEROUS TO GET.
AND I DON'T NEED ANY FRIENDS.
I'M JUST GOING TO TEACH YOU A FEW RULES SO YOU DON'T KILL YOURSELF. THEN YOU'LL BE ON YOUR WAY AND WON'T BOTHER ME AGAIN.
DEAL?
OKAY JEEZ, DEAL...

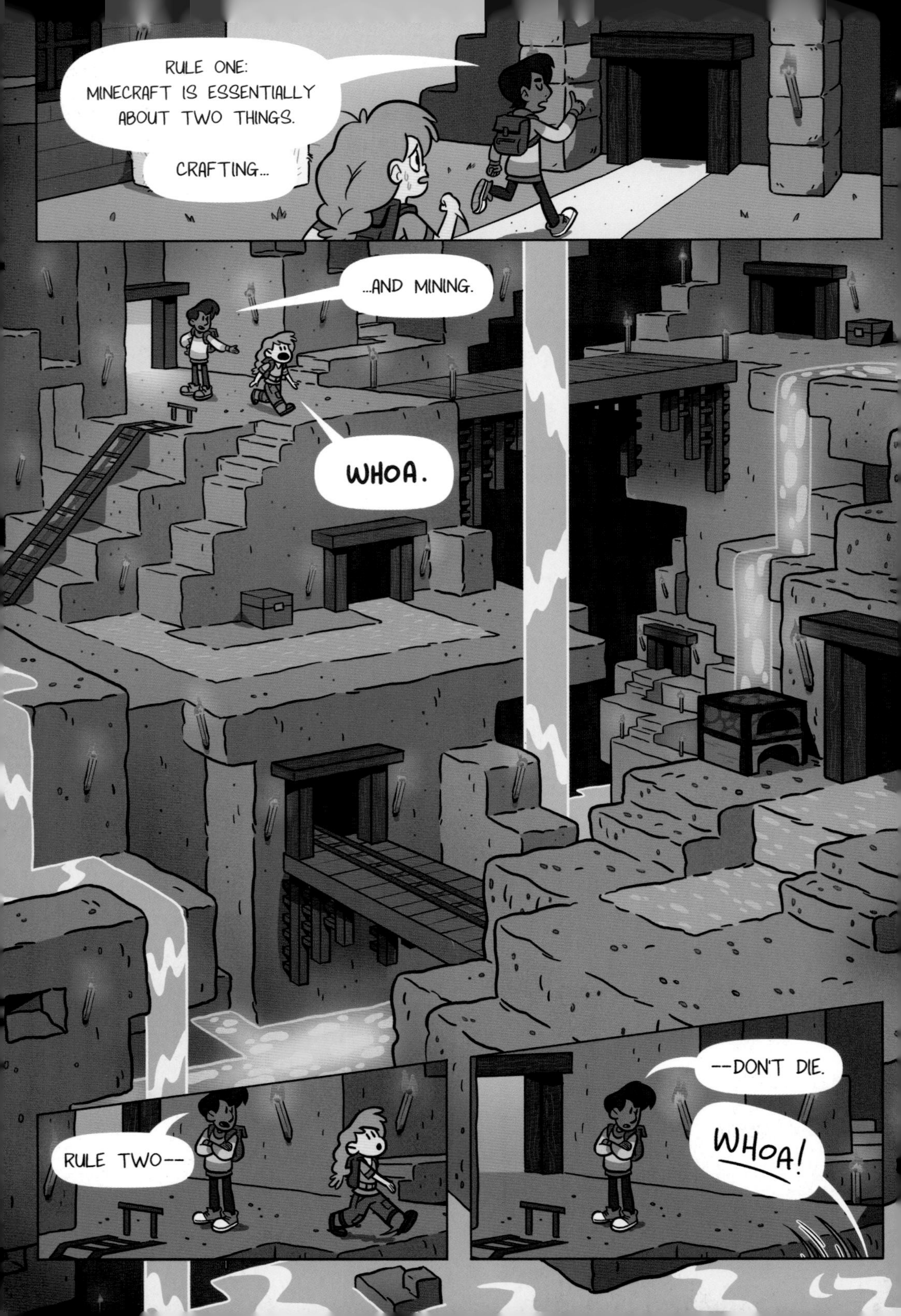
RULE ONE:
MINECRAFT IS ESSENTIALLY ABOUT TWO THINGS.
CRAFTING...
...AND MINING.
WHOA.
RULE TWO--
--DON'T DIE.
WHOA!

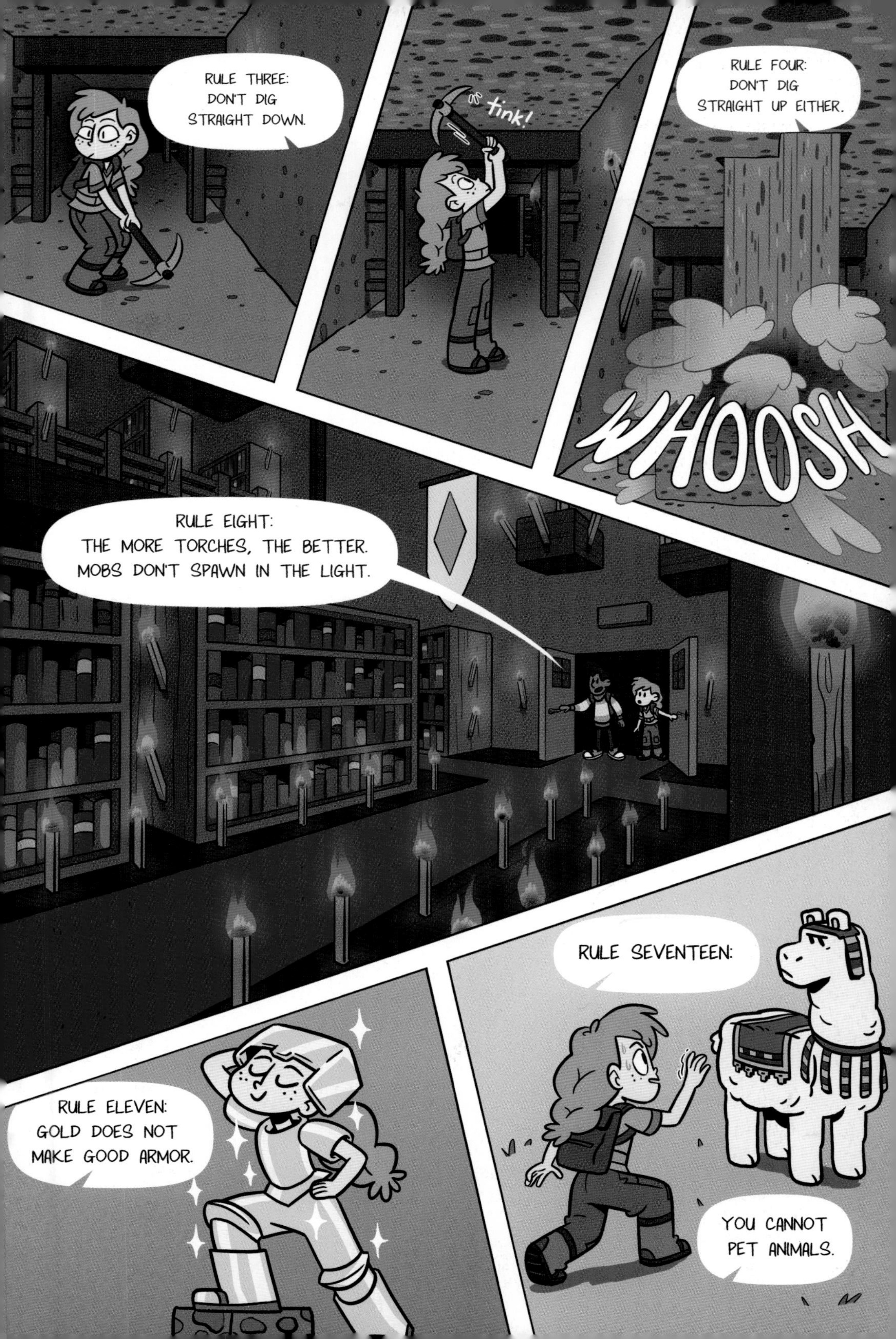
RULE THREE: DON'T DIG STRAIGHT DOWN.
tink!
RULE FOUR: DON'T DIG STRAIGHT UP EITHER.
WHOOSH
RULE EIGHT: THE MORE TORCHES, THE BETTER. MOBS DON'T SPAWN IN THE LIGHT.
RULE ELEVEN: GOLD DOES NOT MAKE GOOD ARMOR.
RULE SEVENTEEN:
YOU CANNOT PET ANIMALS.

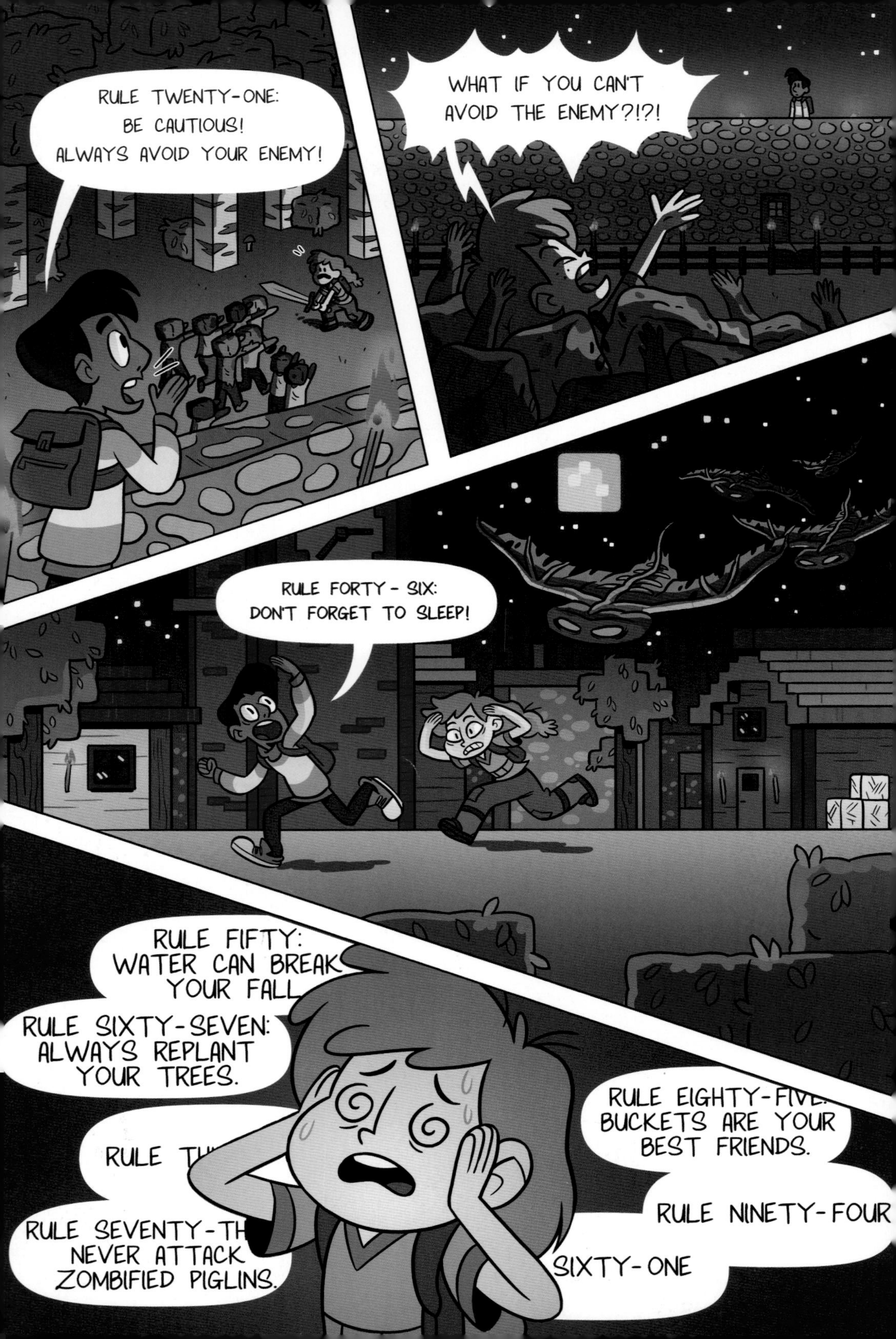
RULE TWENTY-ONE: BE CAUTIOUS! ALWAYS AVOID YOUR ENEMY!
WHAT IF YOU CAN'T AVOID THE ENEMY?!?!
RULE FORTY- SIX: DON'T FORGET TO SLEEP!
RULE FIFTY: WATER CAN BREAK YOUR FALL
RULE SIXTY-SEVEN: ALWAYS REPLANT YOUR TREES.
RULE EIGHTY-FIVE: BUCKETS ARE YOUR BEST FRIENDS.
RULE
RULE NINETY-FOUR
RULE SEVENTY-TH NEVER ATTACK ZOMBIFIED PIGLINS.
SIXTY-ONE

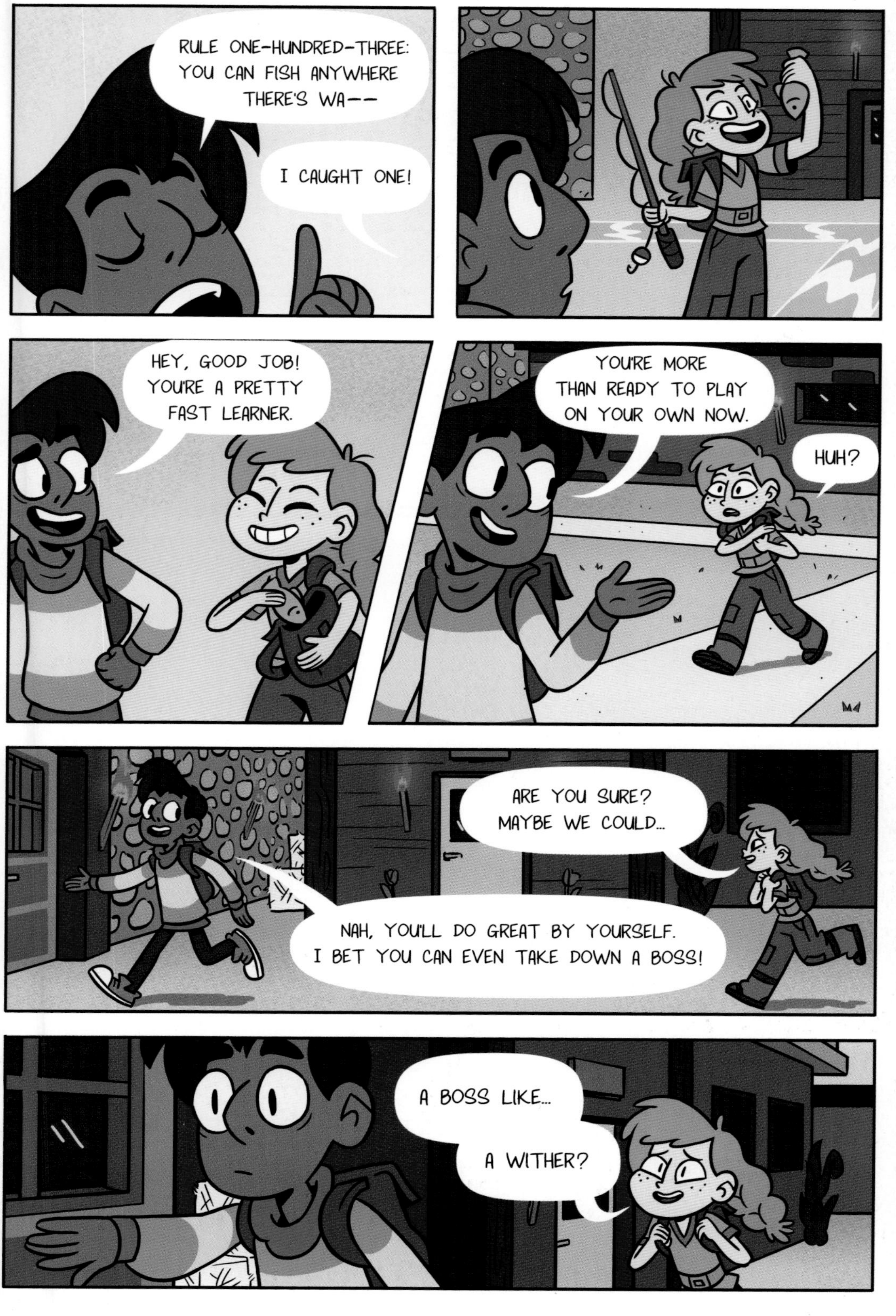
RULE ONE-HUNDRED-THREE: YOU CAN FISH ANYWHERE THERE'S WA--
I CAUGHT ONE!
HEY, GOOD JOB! YOU'RE A PRETTY FAST LEARNER.
YOU'RE MORE THAN READY TO PLAY ON YOUR OWN NOW.
HUH?
ARE YOU SURE? MAYBE WE COULD...
NAH, YOU'LL DO GREAT BY YOURSELF. I BET YOU CAN EVEN TAKE DOWN A BOSS!
A BOSS LIKE...
A WITHER?

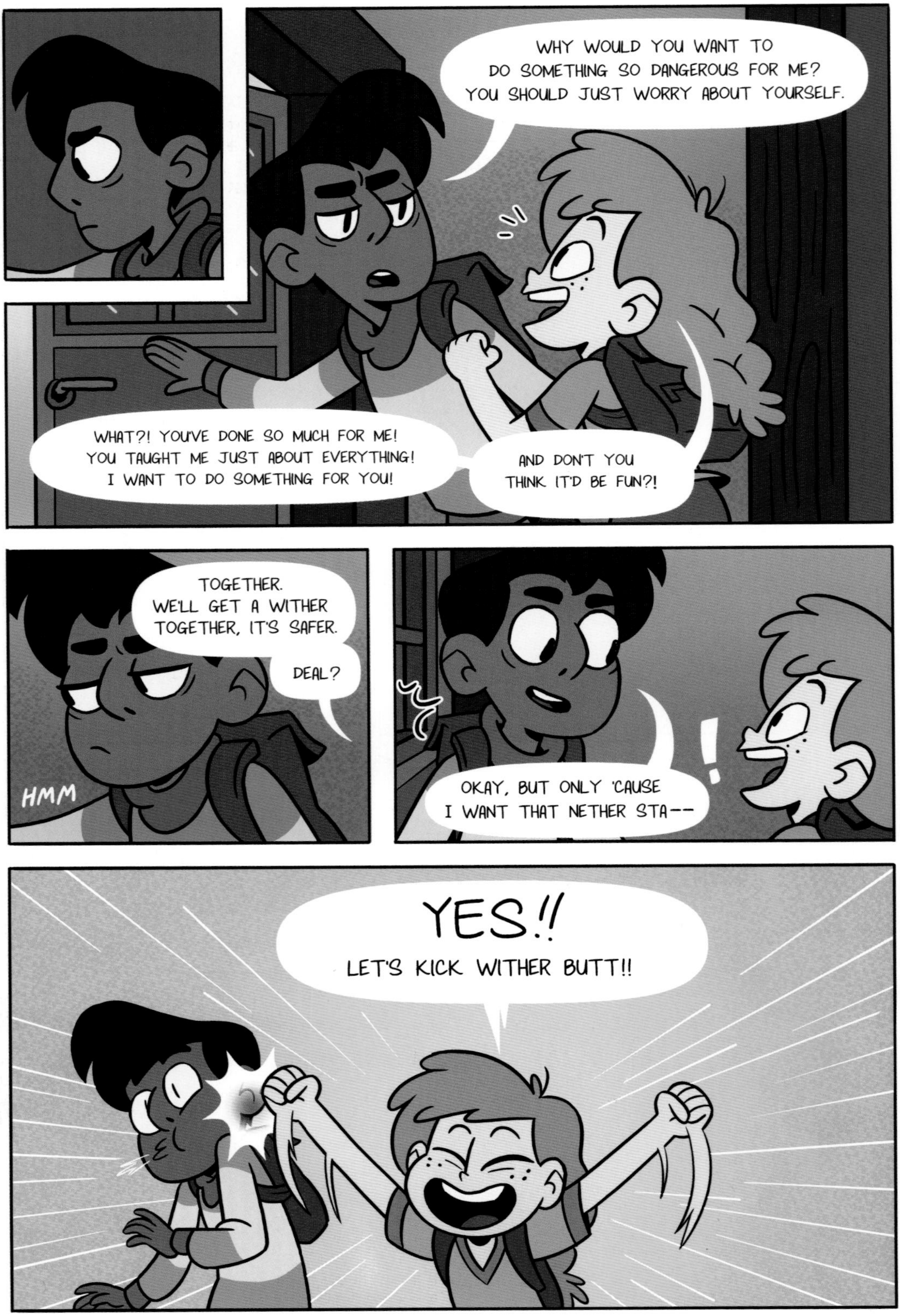
WHY WOULD YOU WANT TO DO SOMETHING SO DANGEROUS FOR ME? YOU SHOULD JUST WORRY ABOUT YOURSELF.
WHAT?! YOU'VE DONE SO MUCH FOR ME! YOU TAUGHT ME JUST ABOUT EVERYTHING! I WANT TO DO SOMETHING FOR YOU!
AND DON'T YOU THINK IT'D BE FUN?!
TOGETHER. WE'LL GET A WITHER TOGETHER, IT'S SAFER.
DEAL?
HMM
OKAY, BUT ONLY 'CAUSE I WANT THAT NETHER STA--
!
YES!!
LET'S KICK WITHER BUTT!!

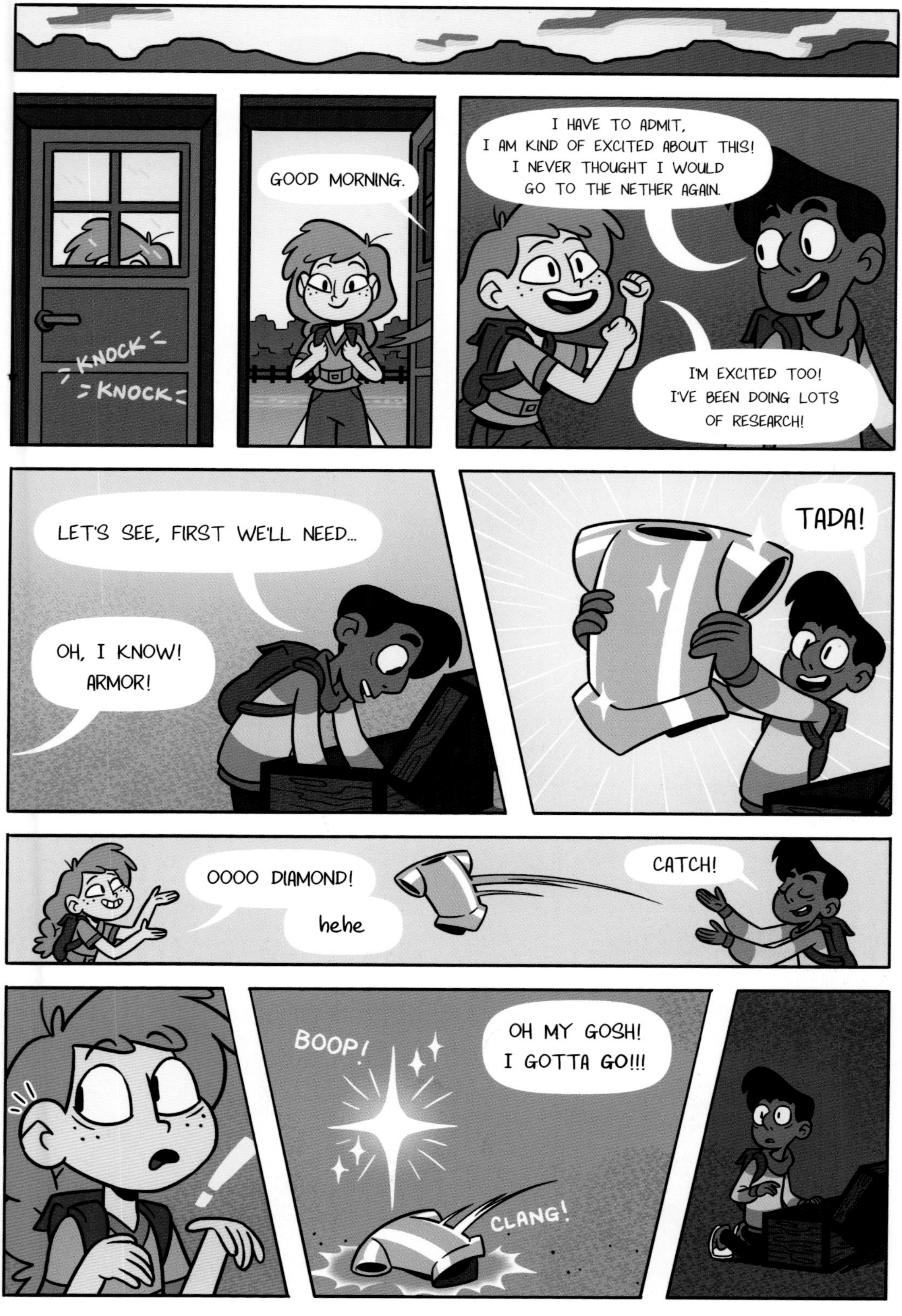
KNOCK
KNOCK
GOOD MORNING.
I HAVE TO ADMIT, I AM KIND OF EXCITED ABOUT THIS! I NEVER THOUGHT I WOULD GO TO THE NETHER AGAIN.
I'M EXCITED TOO! I'VE BEEN DOING LOTS OF RESEARCH!
LET'S SEE, FIRST WE'LL NEED...
OH, I KNOW! ARMOR!
TADA!
OOOO DIAMOND!
hehe
CATCH!
BOOP!
OH MY GOSH! I GOTTA GO!!!
CLANG!

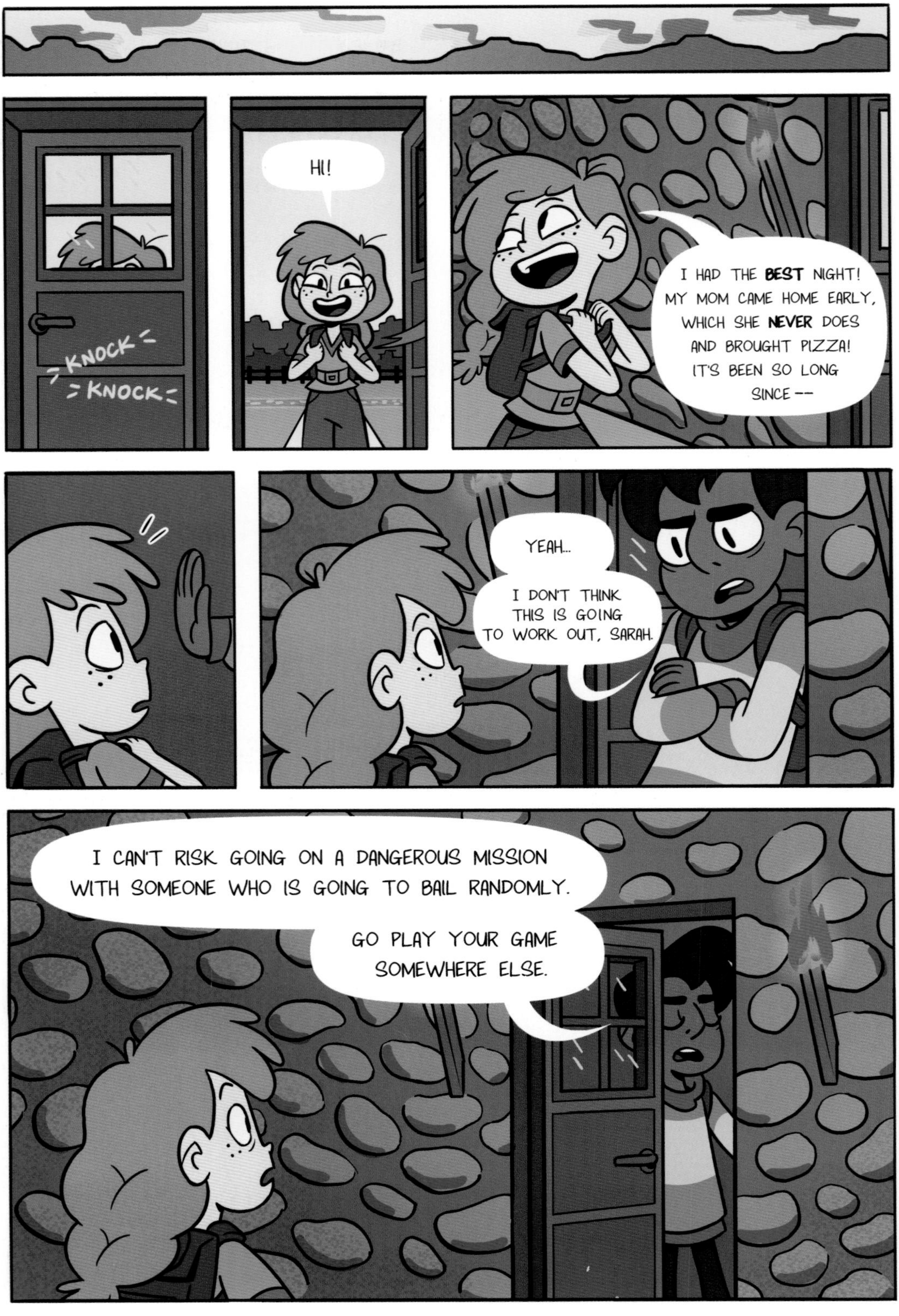
KNOCK
KNOCK
HI!
I HAD THE **BEST** NIGHT! MY MOM CAME HOME EARLY, WHICH SHE **NEVER** DOES AND BROUGHT PIZZA! IT'S BEEN SO LONG SINCE --
YEAH...
I DON'T THINK THIS IS GOING TO WORK OUT, SARAH.
I CAN'T RISK GOING ON A DANGEROUS MISSION WITH SOMEONE WHO IS GOING TO BAIL RANDOMLY.
GO PLAY YOUR GAME SOMEWHERE ELSE.

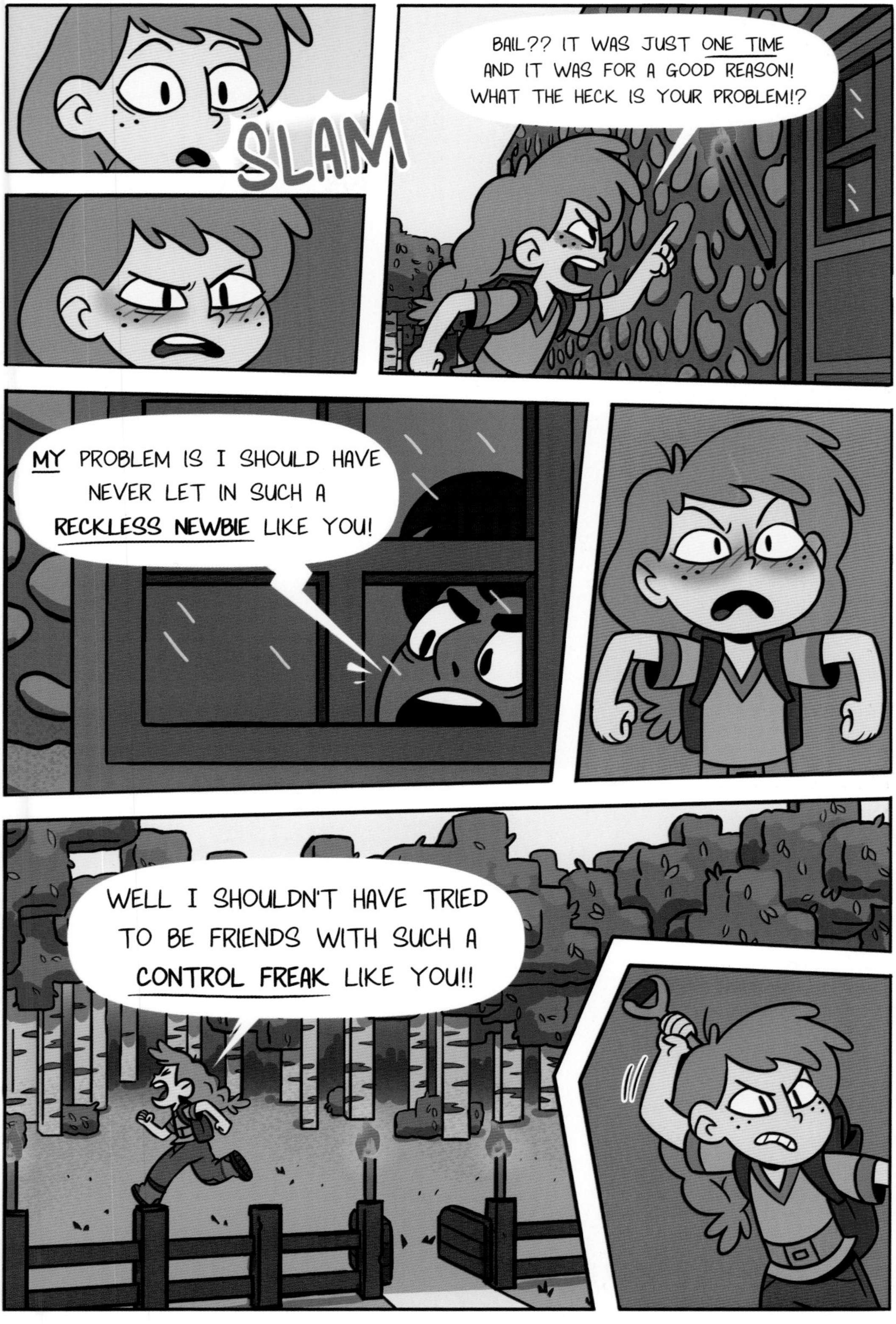
SLAM
BAIL?? IT WAS JUST ONE TIME AND IT WAS FOR A GOOD REASON! WHAT THE HECK IS YOUR PROBLEM!?
MY PROBLEM IS I SHOULD HAVE NEVER LET IN SUCH A RECKLESS NEWBIE LIKE YOU!
WELL I SHOULDN'T HAVE TRIED TO BE FRIENDS WITH SUCH A CONTROL FREAK LIKE YOU!!

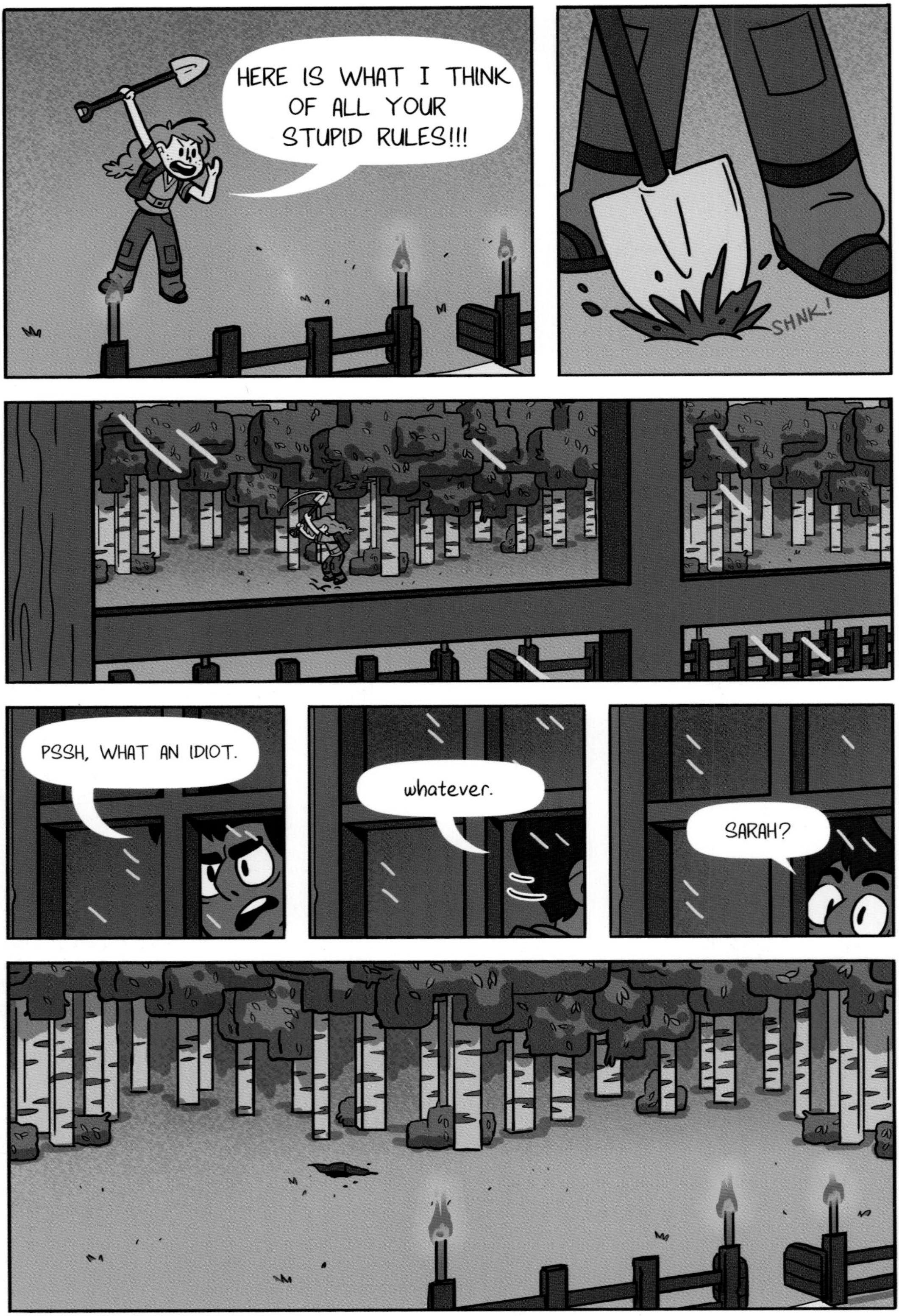
HERE IS WHAT I THINK OF ALL YOUR STUPID RULES!!!
SHNK!
PSSH, WHAT AN IDIOT.
whatever.
SARAH?

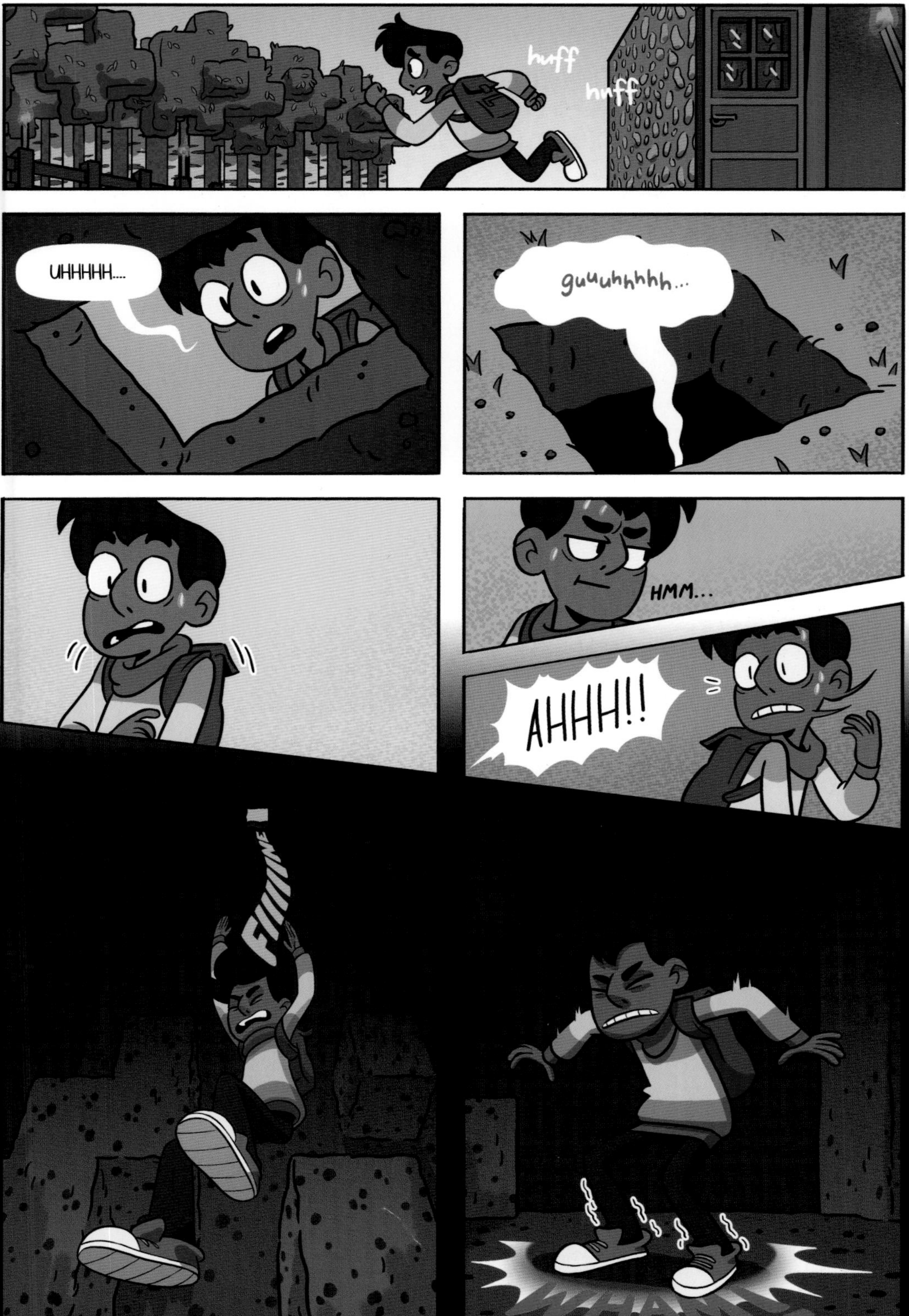
huff
huff
UHHHHH....
guuuhhhhh...
HMM...
AHHH!!
FWHHM
WHAM!

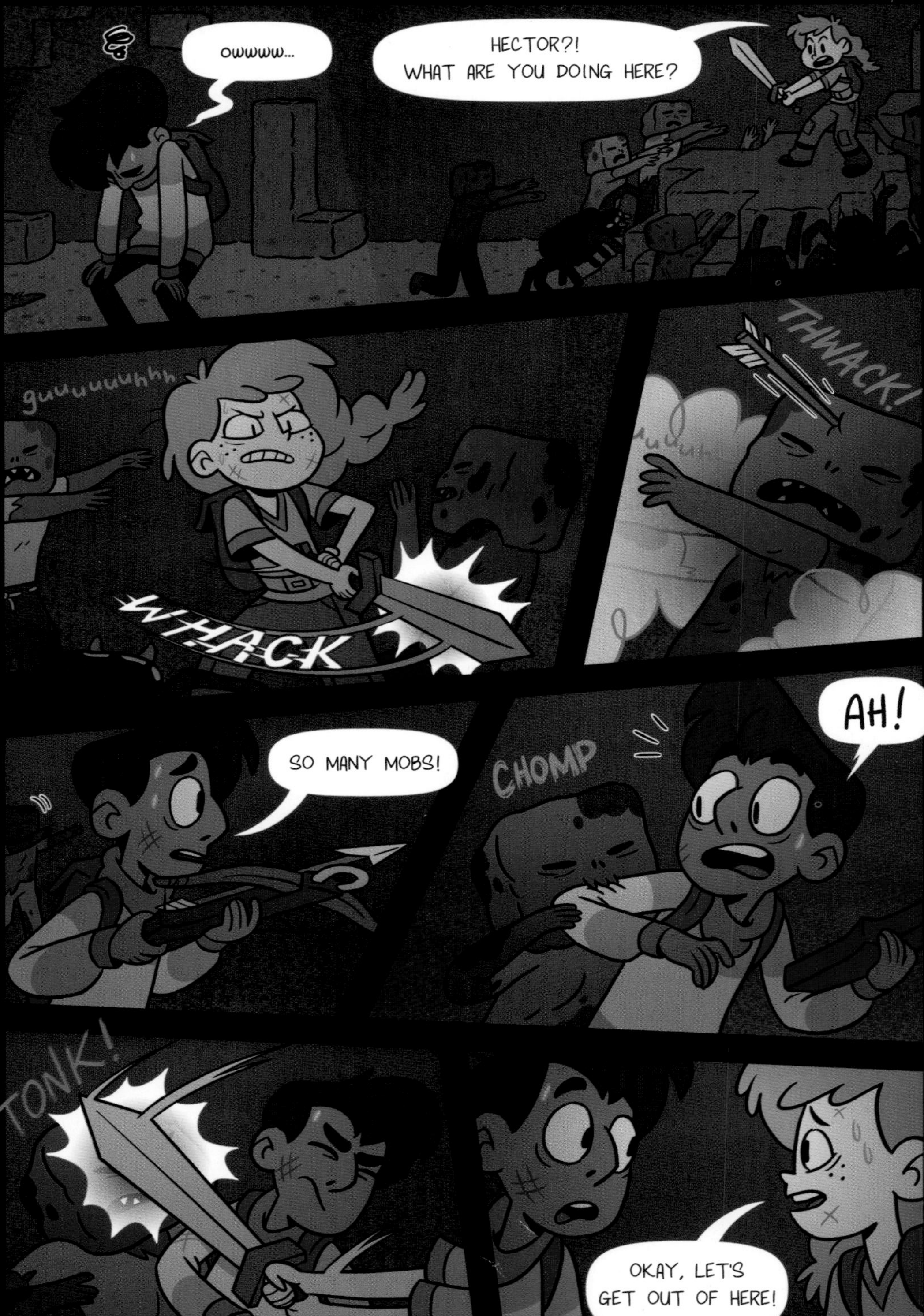
owwww...
HECTOR?!
WHAT ARE YOU DOING HERE?
guuuuuuhhh
WHACK
THWACK!
SO MANY MOBS!
CHOMP
AH!
TONK!
OKAY, LET'S
GET OUT OF HERE!

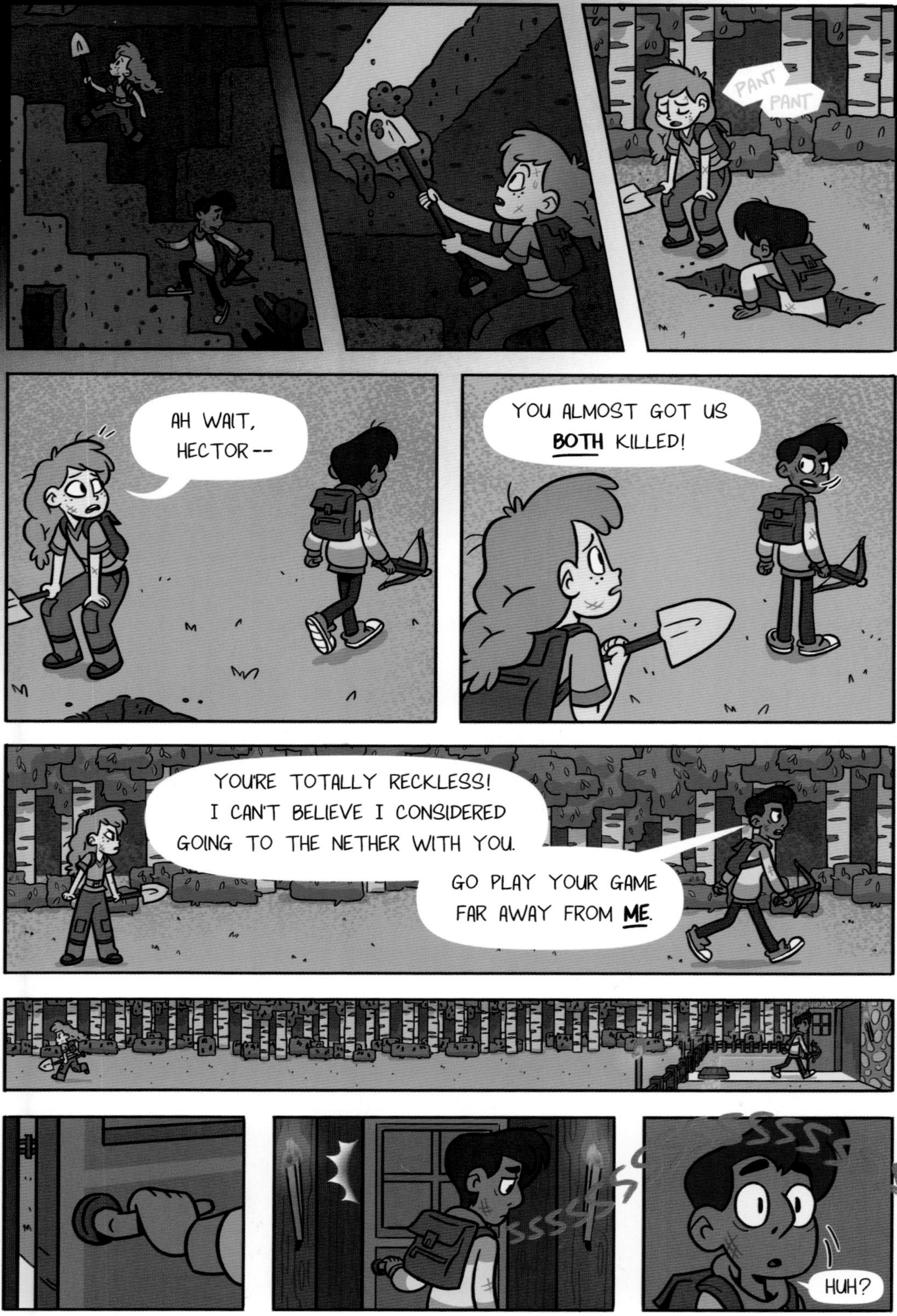
PANT
PANT
AH WAIT, HECTOR--
YOU ALMOST GOT US **BOTH** KILLED!
YOU'RE TOTALLY RECKLESS! I CAN'T BELIEVE I CONSIDERED GOING TO THE NETHER WITH YOU.
GO PLAY YOUR GAME FAR AWAY FROM **ME**.
SSSSS
HUH?

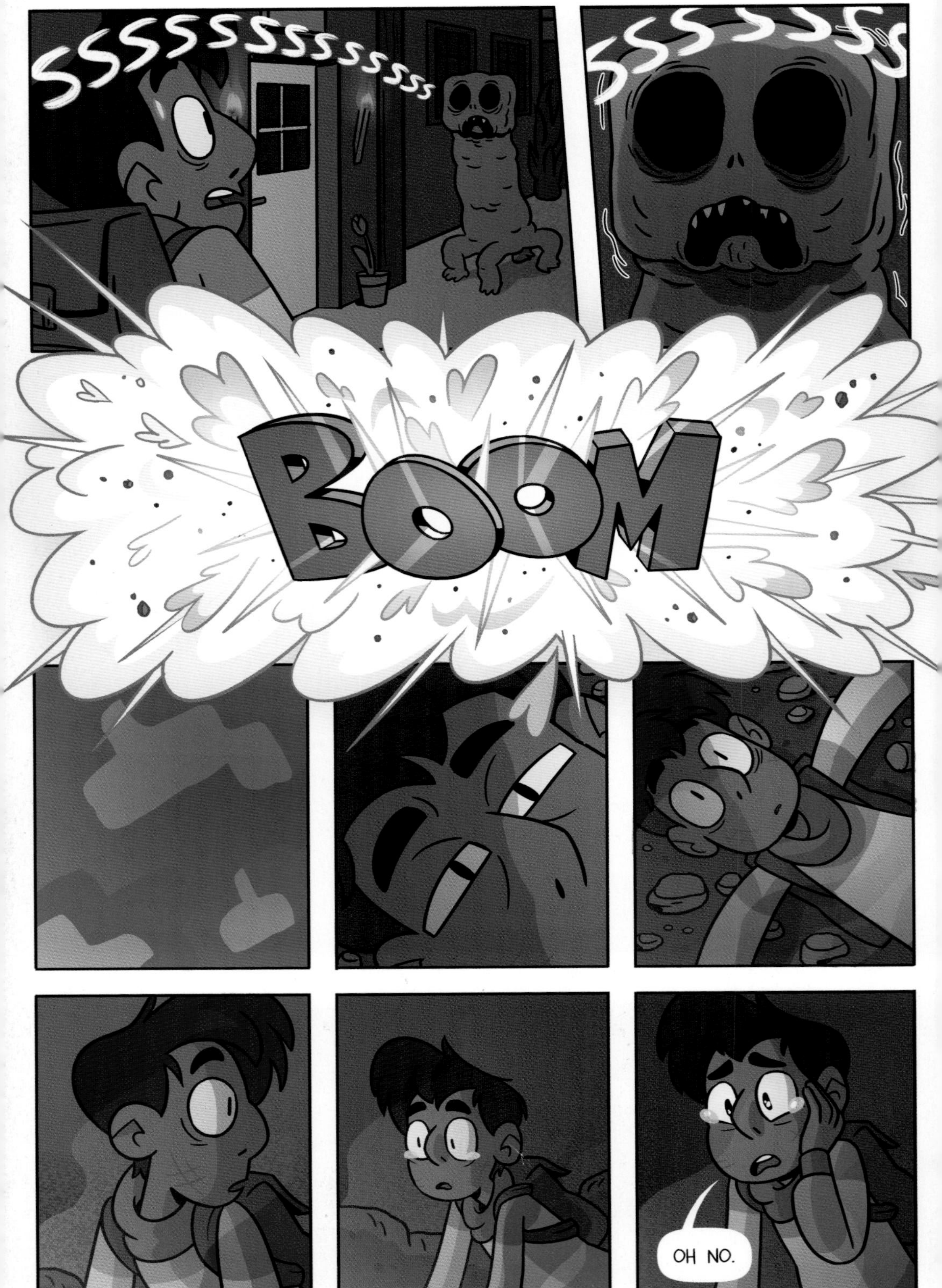
SSSSSSSSSSSSSSSS
SSSSSSS
BOOM
OH NO.

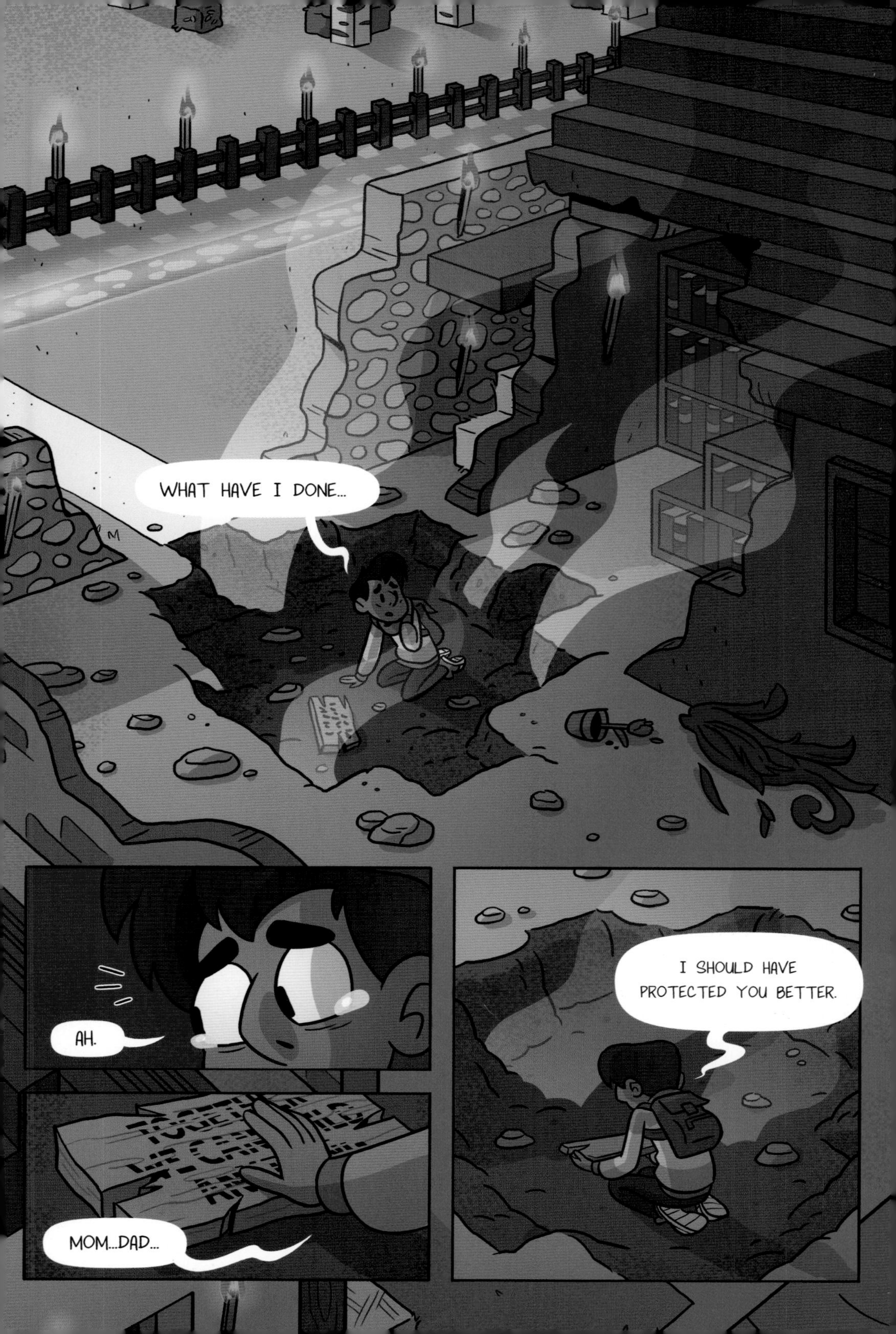
WHAT HAVE I DONE...
AH.
MOM...DAD...
I SHOULD HAVE PROTECTED YOU BETTER.

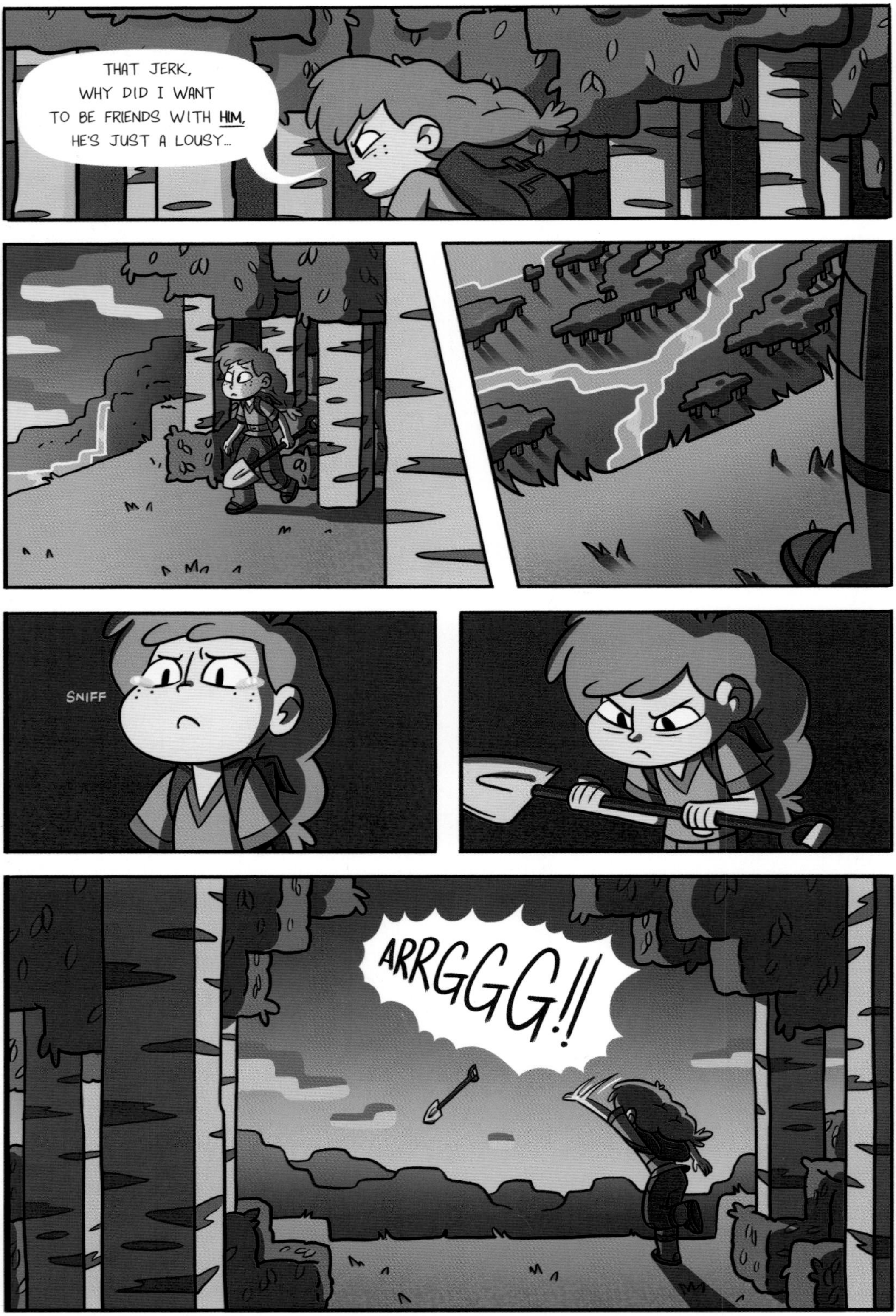
THAT JERK, WHY DID I WANT TO BE FRIENDS WITH HIM, HE'S JUST A LOUSY...
SNIFF
ARRGGG!!

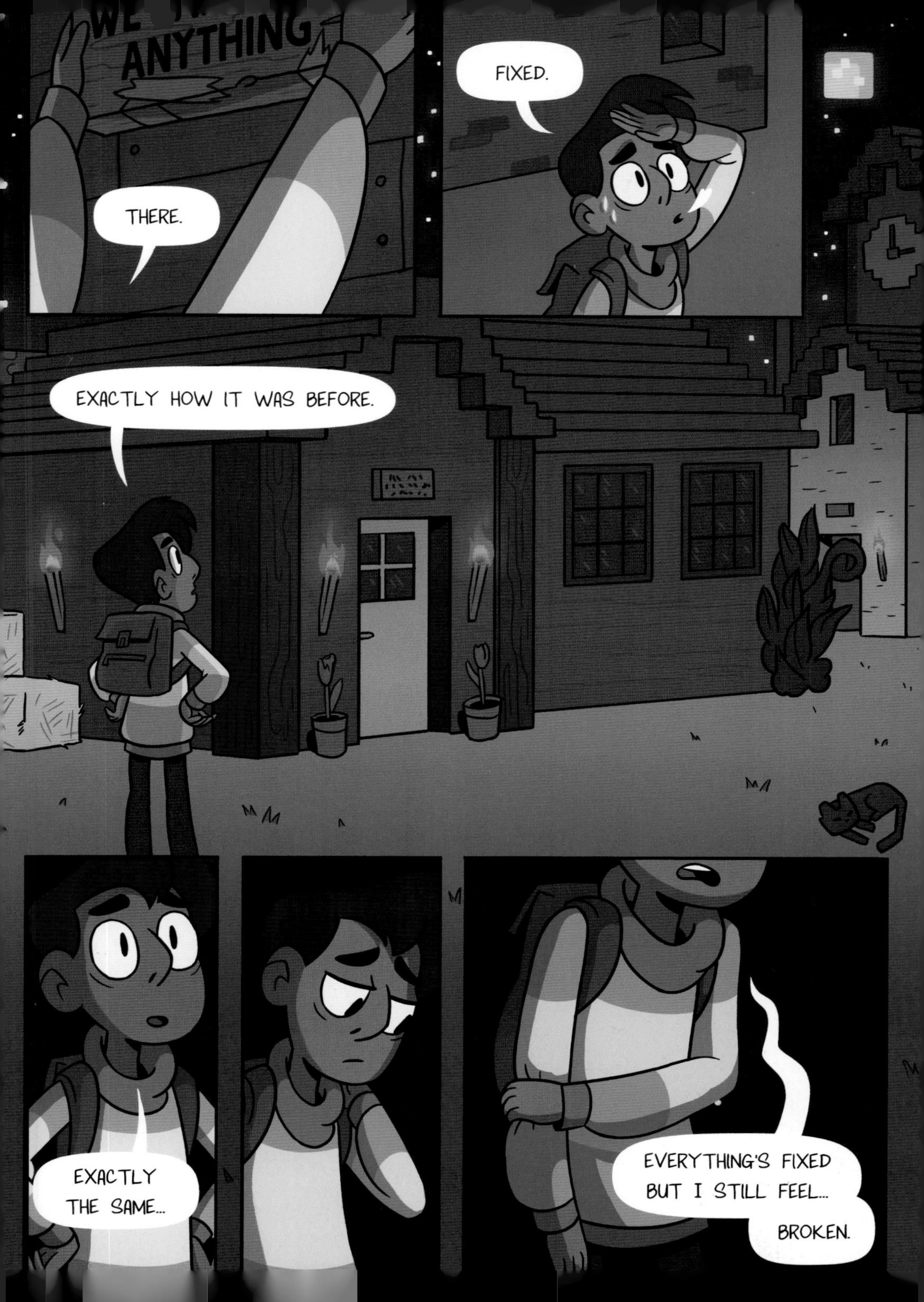

ANYTHING
THERE.
FIXED.
EXACTLY HOW IT WAS BEFORE.
EXACTLY THE SAME...
EVERYTHING'S FIXED BUT I STILL FEEL...
BROKEN.

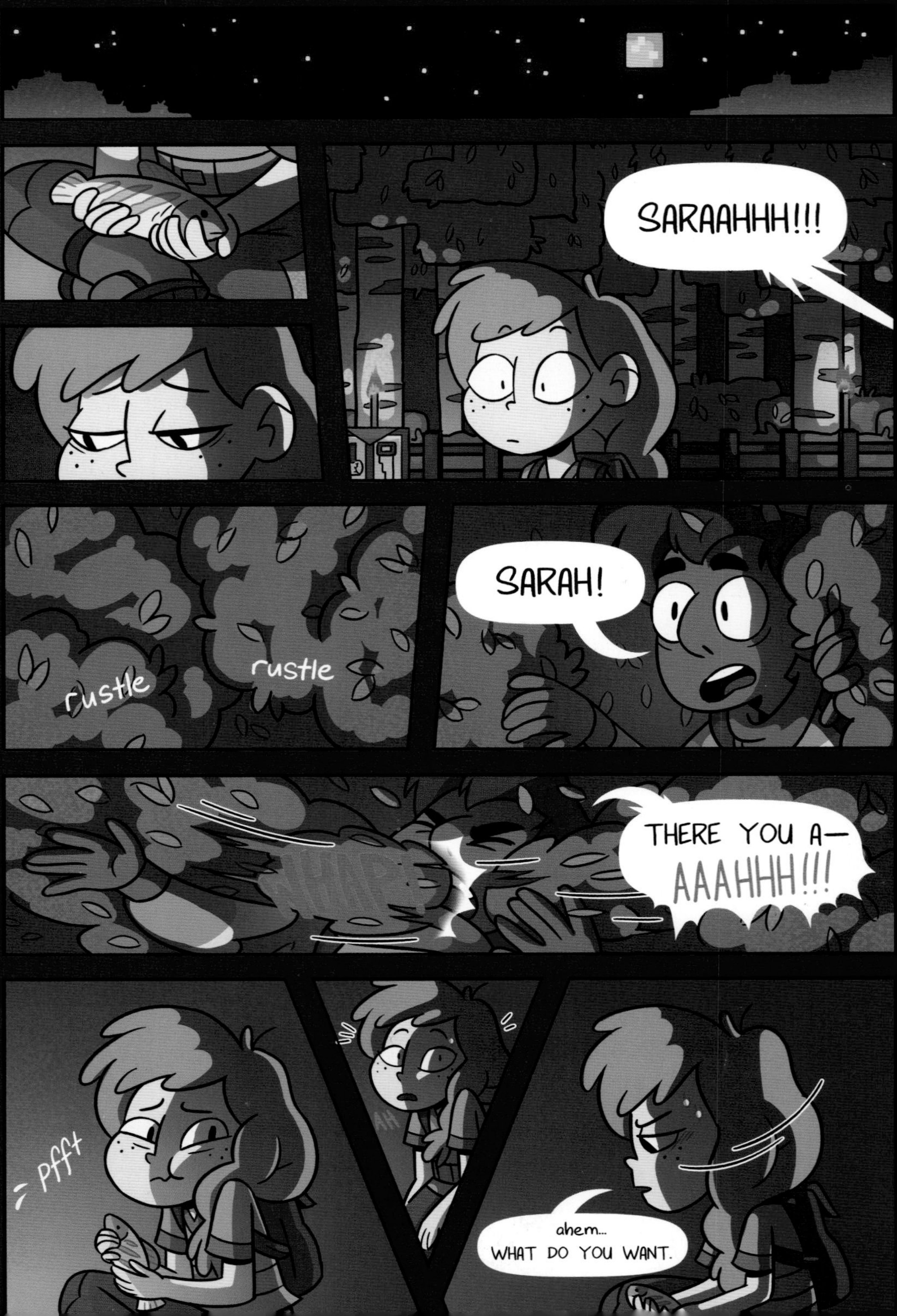
SARAAHHH!!!
SARAH!
rustle
rustle
THERE YOU A—
AAAHHH!!!
pfft
ahem...
WHAT DO YOU WANT.

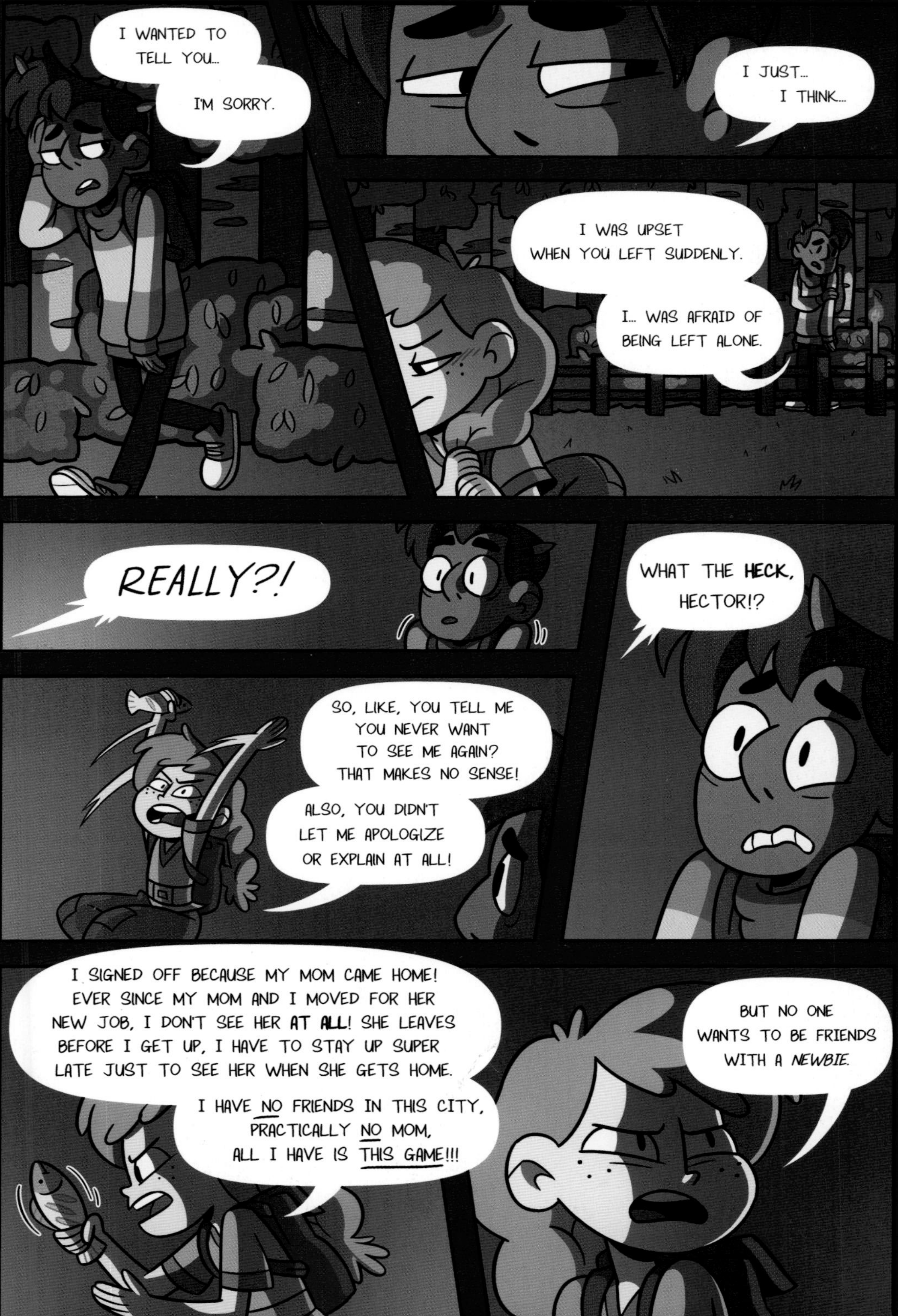
I WANTED TO TELL YOU...
I'M SORRY.
I JUST... I THINK...
I WAS UPSET WHEN YOU LEFT SUDDENLY.
I... WAS AFRAID OF BEING LEFT ALONE.
REALLY?!
WHAT THE **HECK**, HECTOR!?
SO, LIKE, YOU TELL ME YOU NEVER WANT TO SEE ME AGAIN? THAT MAKES NO SENSE!
ALSO, YOU DIDN'T LET ME APOLOGIZE OR EXPLAIN AT ALL!
I SIGNED OFF BECAUSE MY MOM CAME HOME! EVER SINCE MY MOM AND I MOVED FOR HER NEW JOB, I DON'T SEE HER **AT ALL**! SHE LEAVES BEFORE I GET UP, I HAVE TO STAY UP SUPER LATE JUST TO SEE HER WHEN SHE GETS HOME.
I HAVE NO FRIENDS IN THIS CITY, PRACTICALLY NO MOM, ALL I HAVE IS THIS GAME!!!
BUT NO ONE WANTS TO BE FRIENDS WITH A *NEWBIE*.

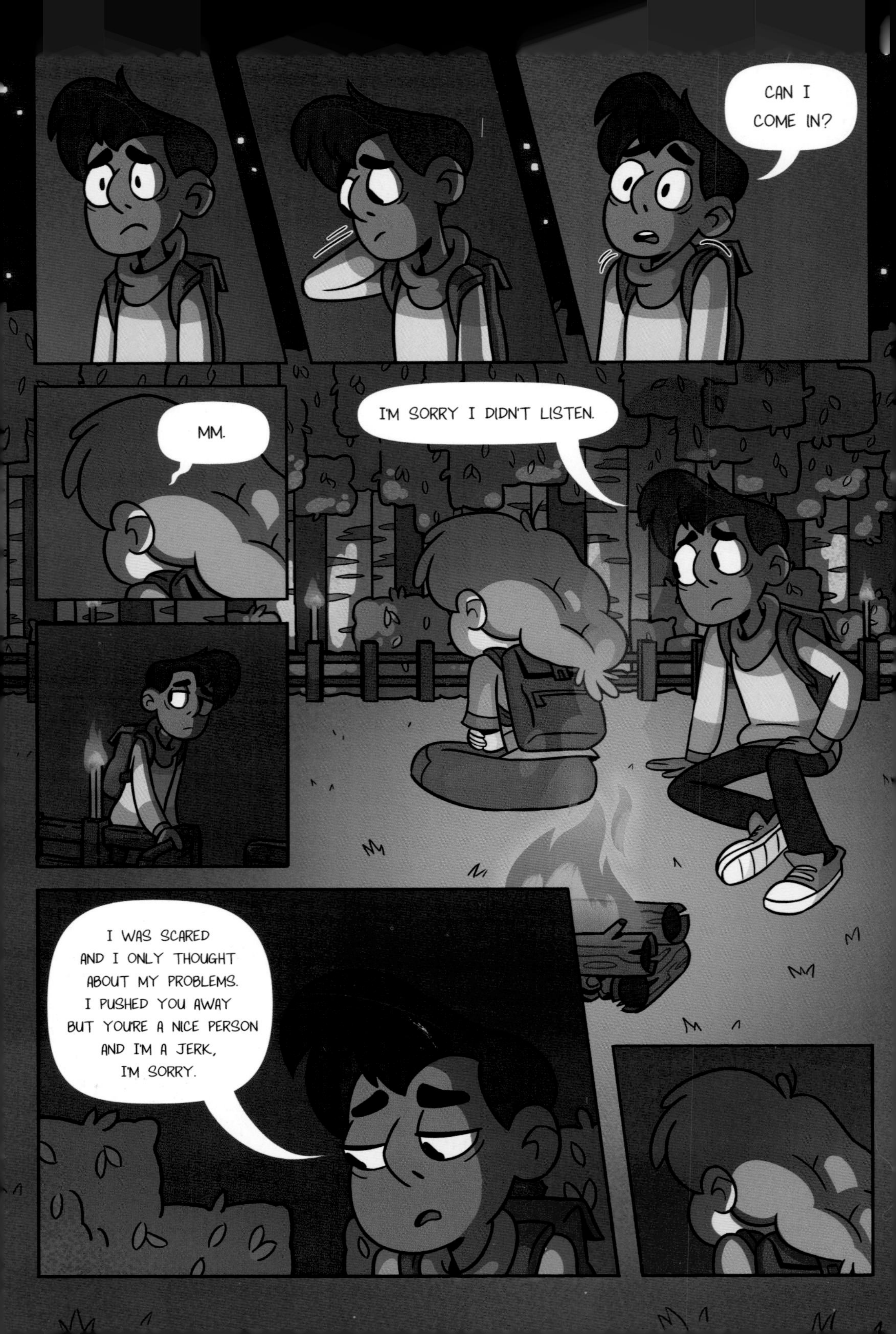

CAN I COME IN?
MM.
I'M SORRY I DIDN'T LISTEN.
I WAS SCARED AND I ONLY THOUGHT ABOUT MY PROBLEMS. I PUSHED YOU AWAY BUT YOU'RE A NICE PERSON AND I'M A JERK, I'M SORRY.

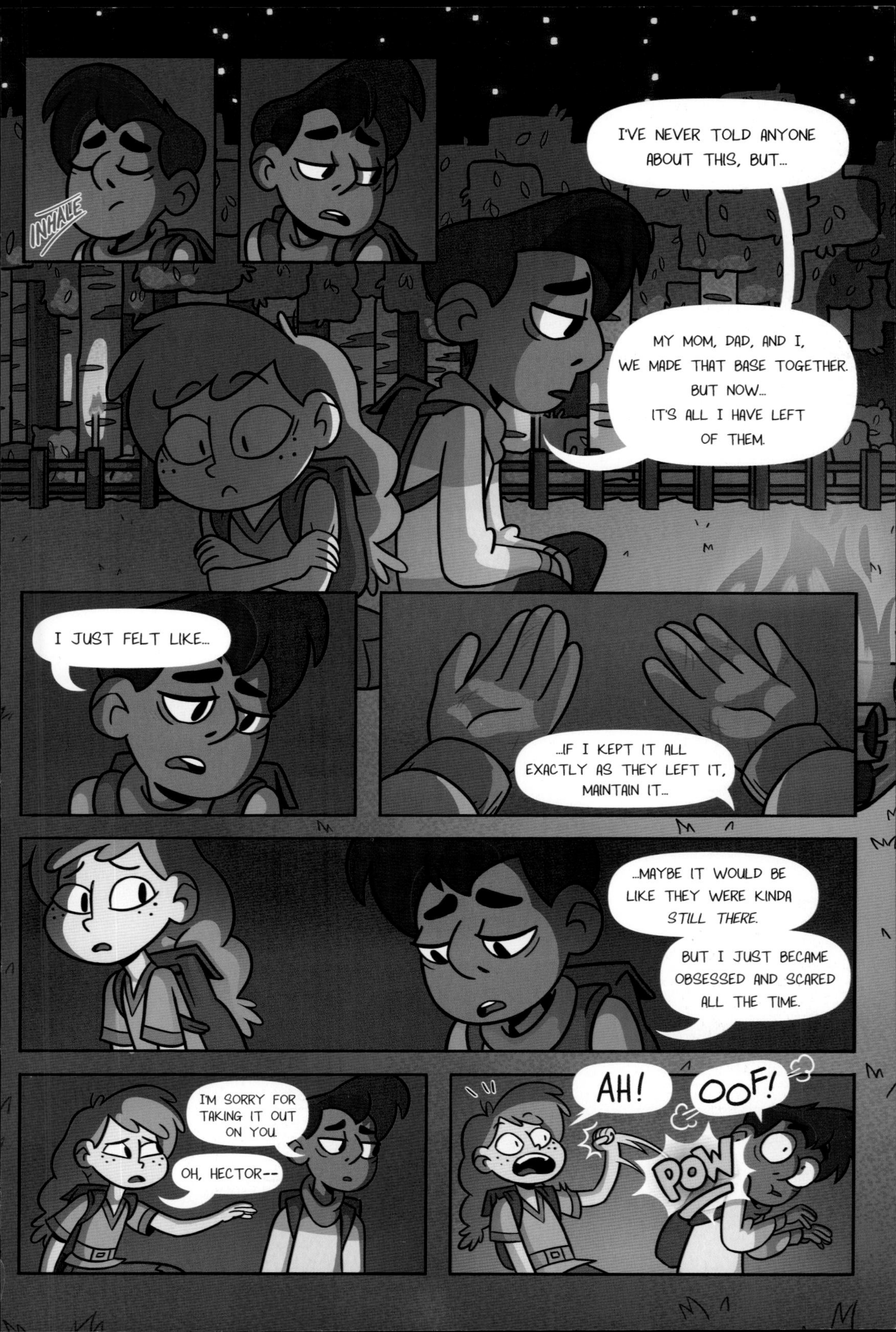
INHALE
I'VE NEVER TOLD ANYONE ABOUT THIS, BUT...
MY MOM, DAD, AND I, WE MADE THAT BASE TOGETHER. BUT NOW... IT'S ALL I HAVE LEFT OF THEM.
I JUST FELT LIKE...
...IF I KEPT IT ALL EXACTLY AS THEY LEFT IT, MAINTAIN IT...
...MAYBE IT WOULD BE LIKE THEY WERE KINDA *STILL THERE.*
BUT I JUST BECAME OBSESSED AND SCARED ALL THE TIME.
I'M SORRY FOR TAKING IT OUT ON YOU.
OH, HECTOR--
AH!
OOF!
POW

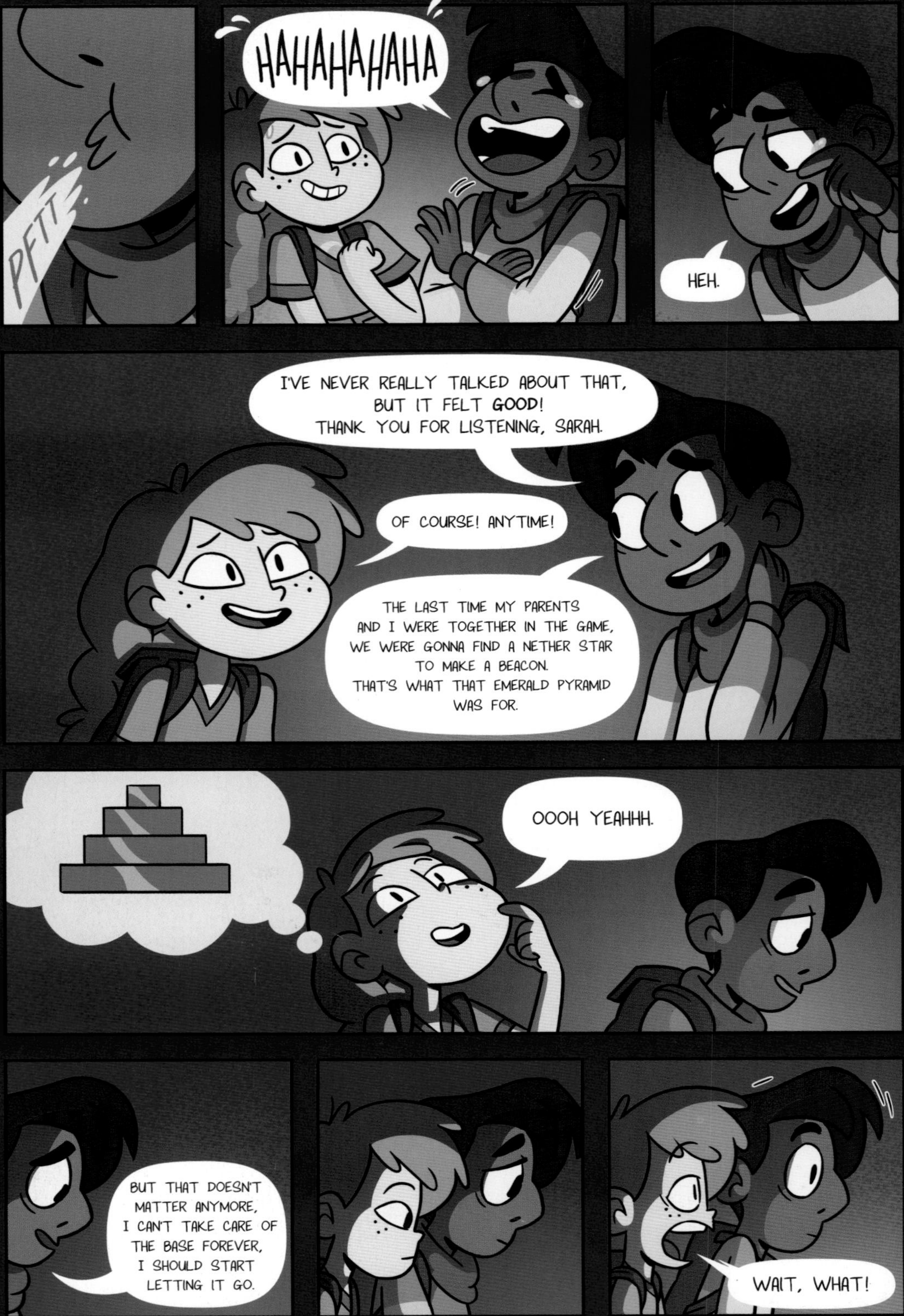
PFTT
HAHAHAHAHA
HEH.
I'VE NEVER REALLY TALKED ABOUT THAT, BUT IT FELT **GOOD**! THANK YOU FOR LISTENING, SARAH.
OF COURSE! ANYTIME!
THE LAST TIME MY PARENTS AND I WERE TOGETHER IN THE GAME, WE WERE GONNA FIND A NETHER STAR TO MAKE A BEACON. THAT'S WHAT THAT EMERALD PYRAMID WAS FOR.
OOOH YEAHHH.
BUT THAT DOESN'T MATTER ANYMORE, I CAN'T TAKE CARE OF THE BASE FOREVER, I SHOULD START LETTING IT GO.
WAIT, WHAT!

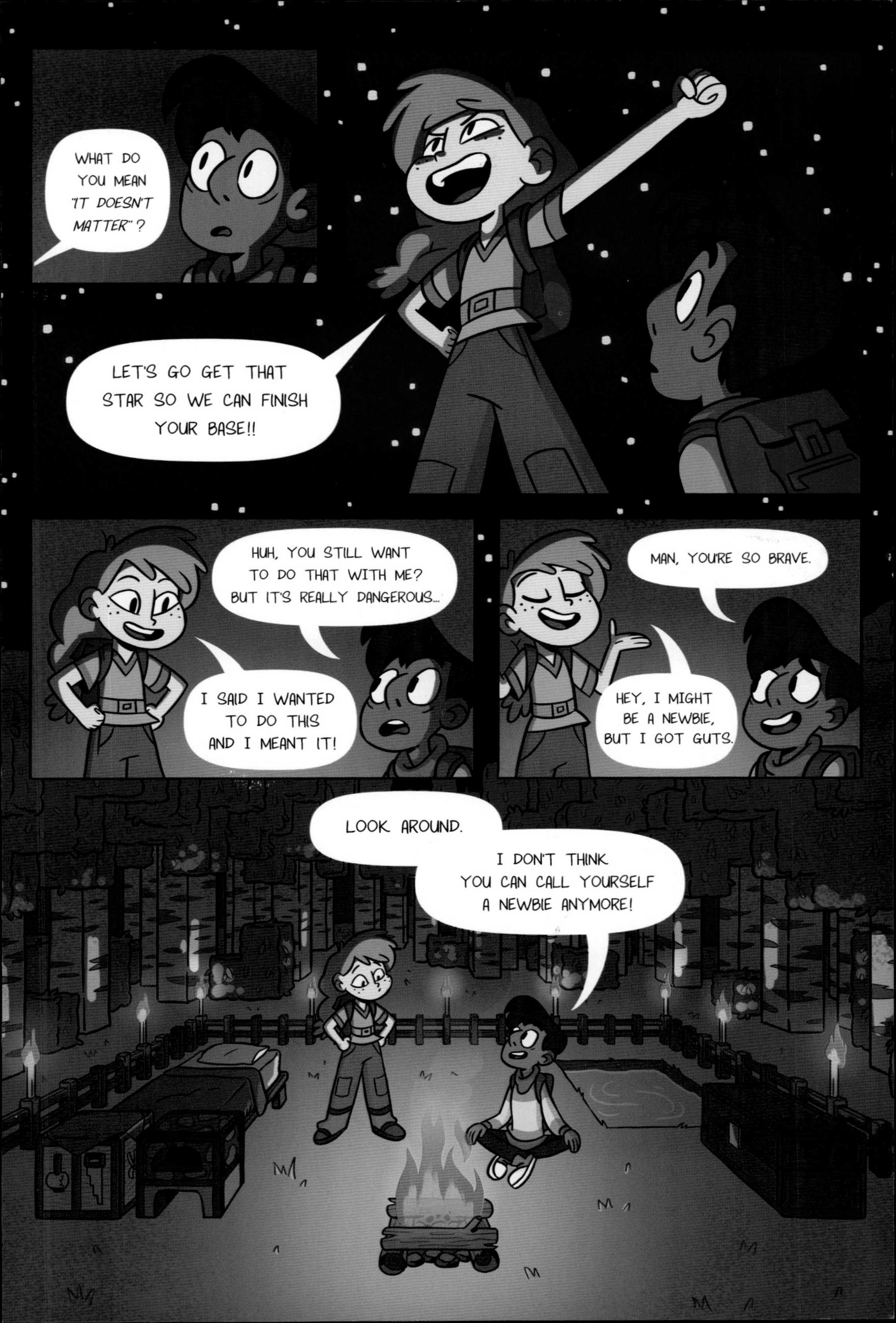
WHAT DO YOU MEAN "IT DOESN'T MATTER"?
LET'S GO GET THAT STAR SO WE CAN FINISH YOUR BASE!!
HUH, YOU STILL WANT TO DO THAT WITH ME? BUT IT'S REALLY DANGEROUS...
I SAID I WANTED TO DO THIS AND I MEANT IT!
MAN, YOU'RE SO BRAVE.
HEY, I MIGHT BE A NEWBIE, BUT I GOT GUTS.
LOOK AROUND.
I DON'T THINK YOU CAN CALL YOURSELF A NEWBIE ANYMORE!

WE HAVE A LOT TO PREPARE.

THE WITHER IS ONE OF THE TOUGHEST BOSSES IN THE GAME.

WE NEED HEALING POTIONS.

BUT BEFORE THE WITHER, WE HAVE TO GO TO THE NETHER. AND IT WILL BE DANGEROUS.

WE NEED THREE WITHER SKELETON SKULLS.

IT WILL BE HARD.

BUT I THINK *WE CAN DO IT.*

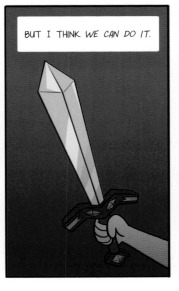

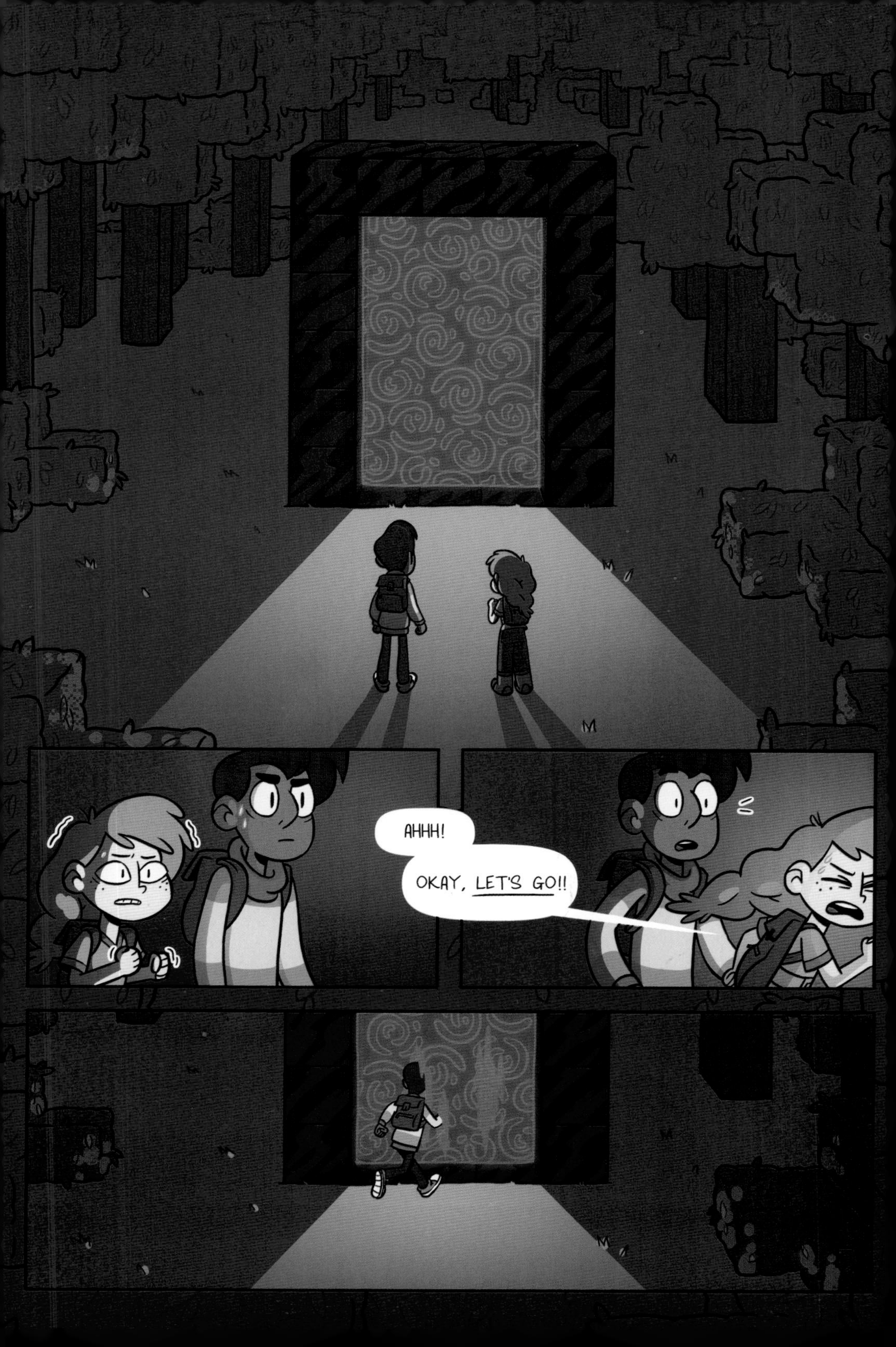
AHHH!
OKAY, LET'S GO!!

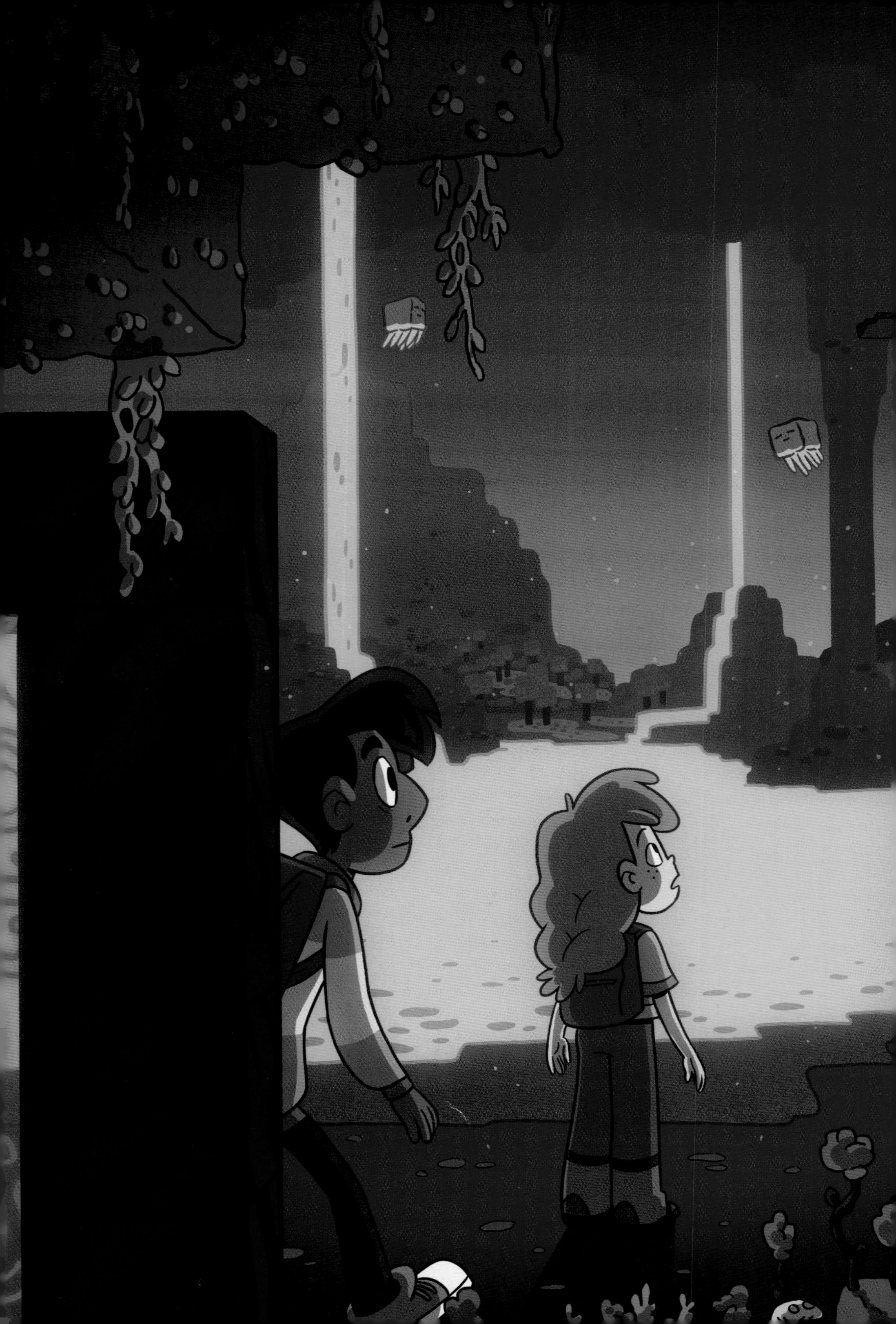

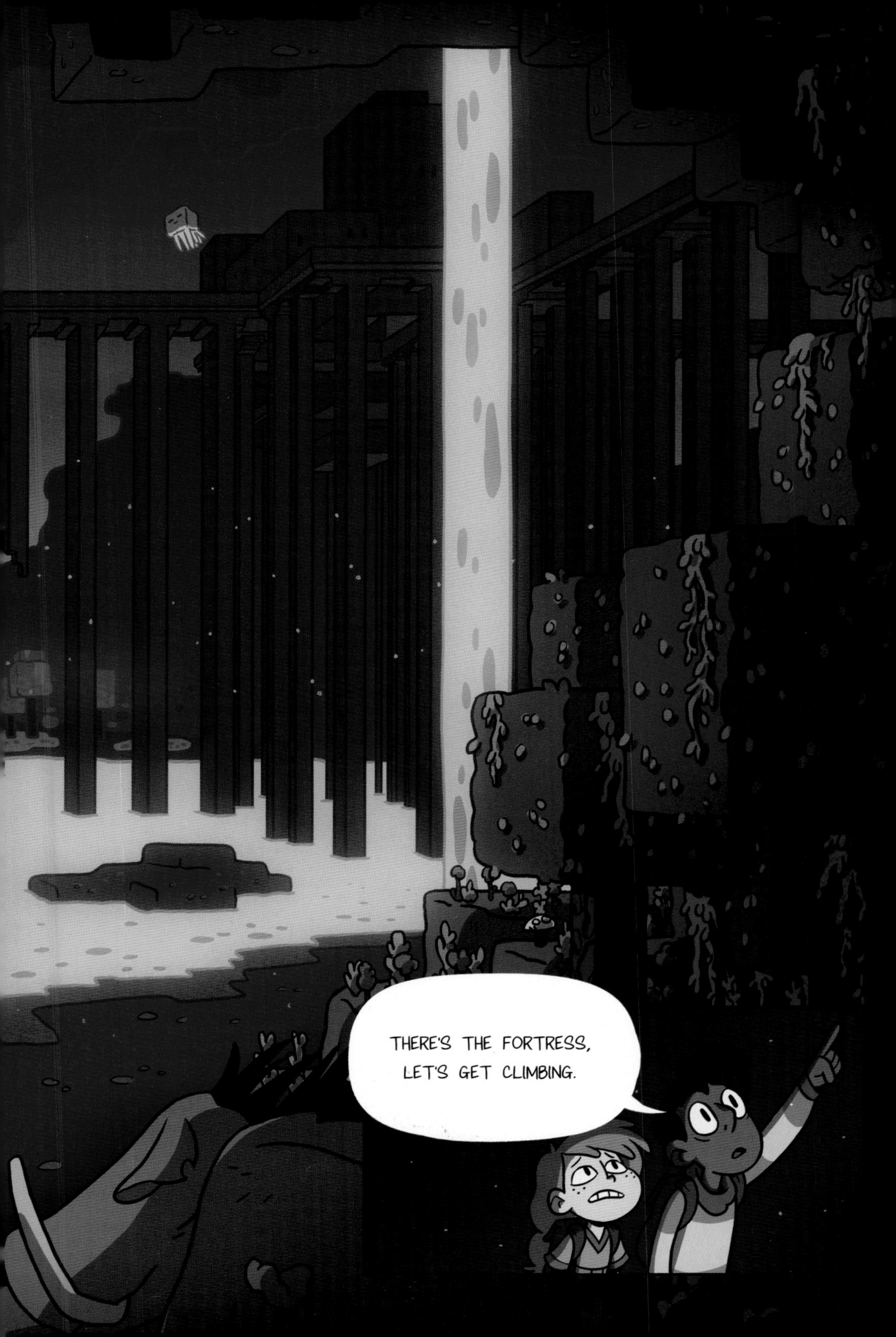
THERE'S THE FORTRESS, LET'S GET CLIMBING.

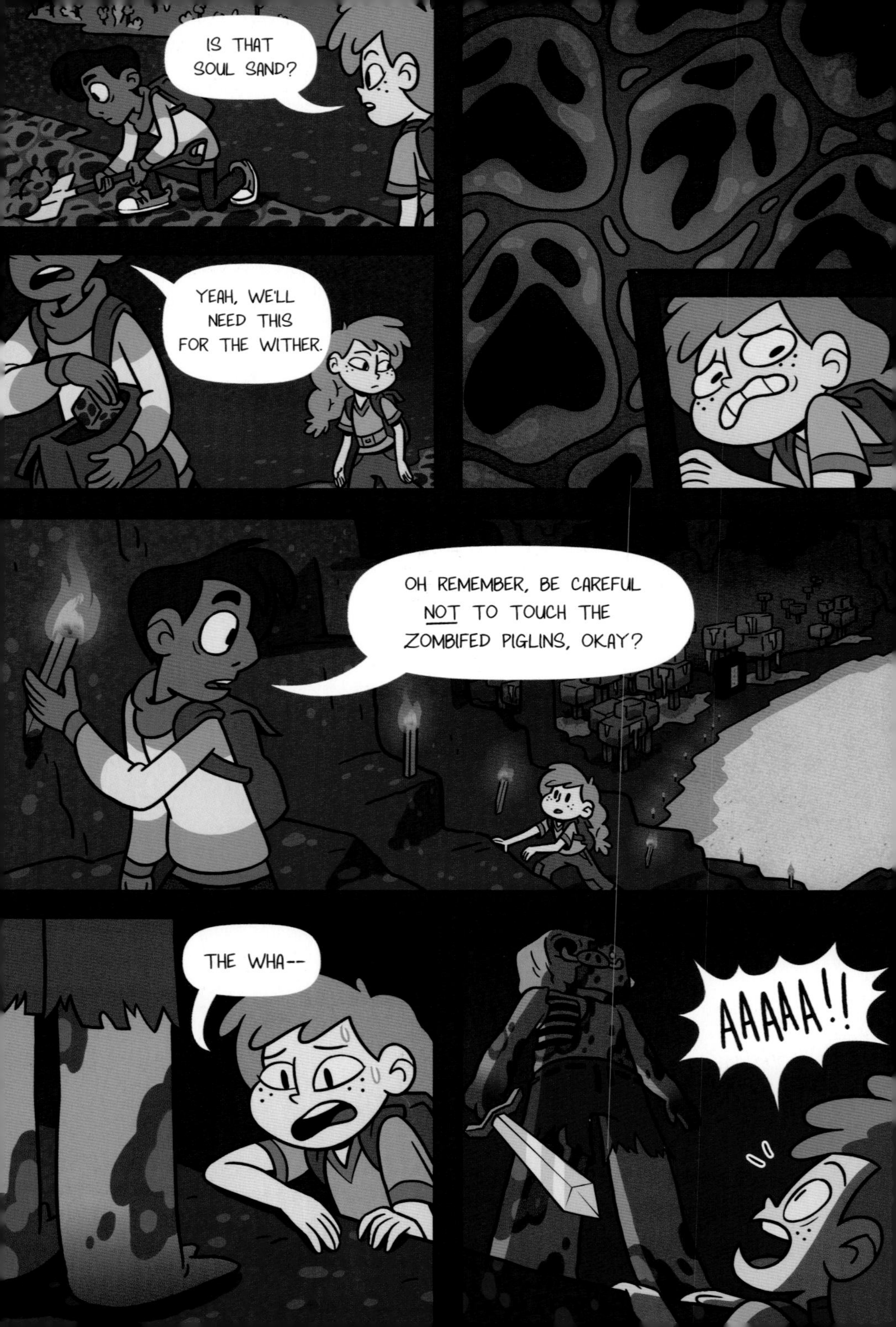
IS THAT SOUL SAND?
YEAH, WE'LL NEED THIS FOR THE WITHER.
OH REMEMBER, BE CAREFUL NOT TO TOUCH THE ZOMBIFED PIGLINS, OKAY?
THE WHA--
AAAAA!!

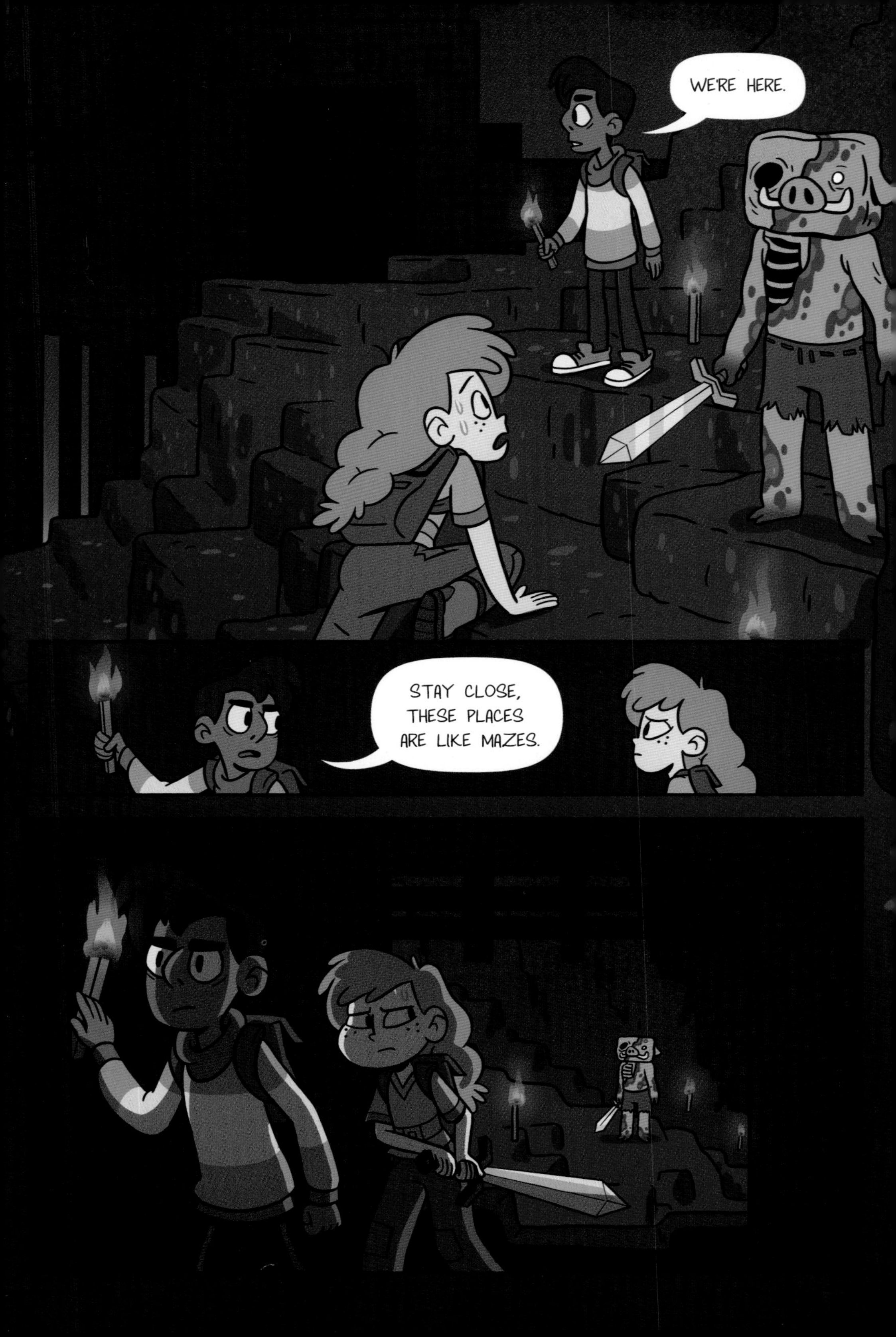
WE'RE HERE.
STAY CLOSE, THESE PLACES ARE LIKE MAZES.

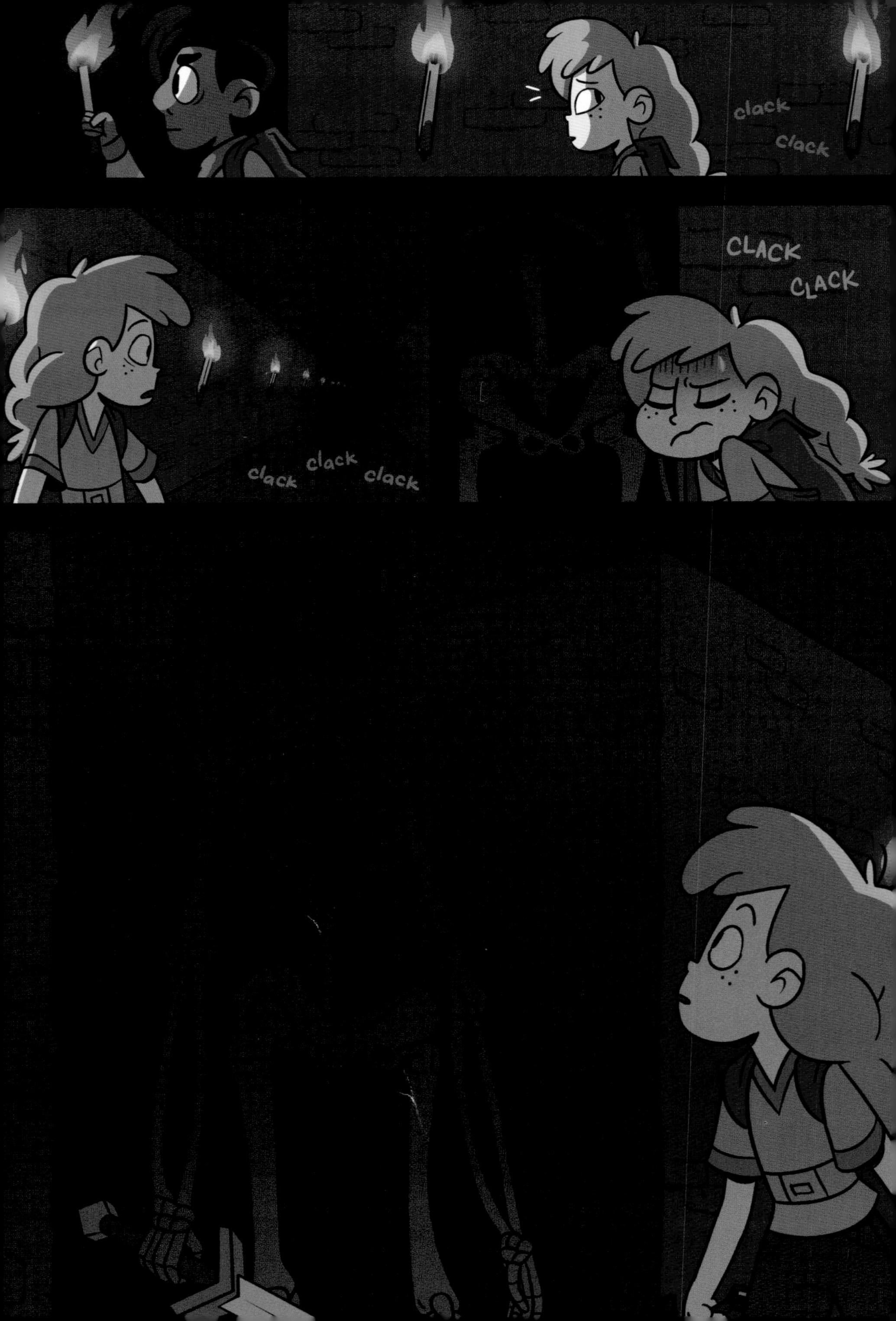
clack
clack
CLACK
CLACK
clack
clack
clack

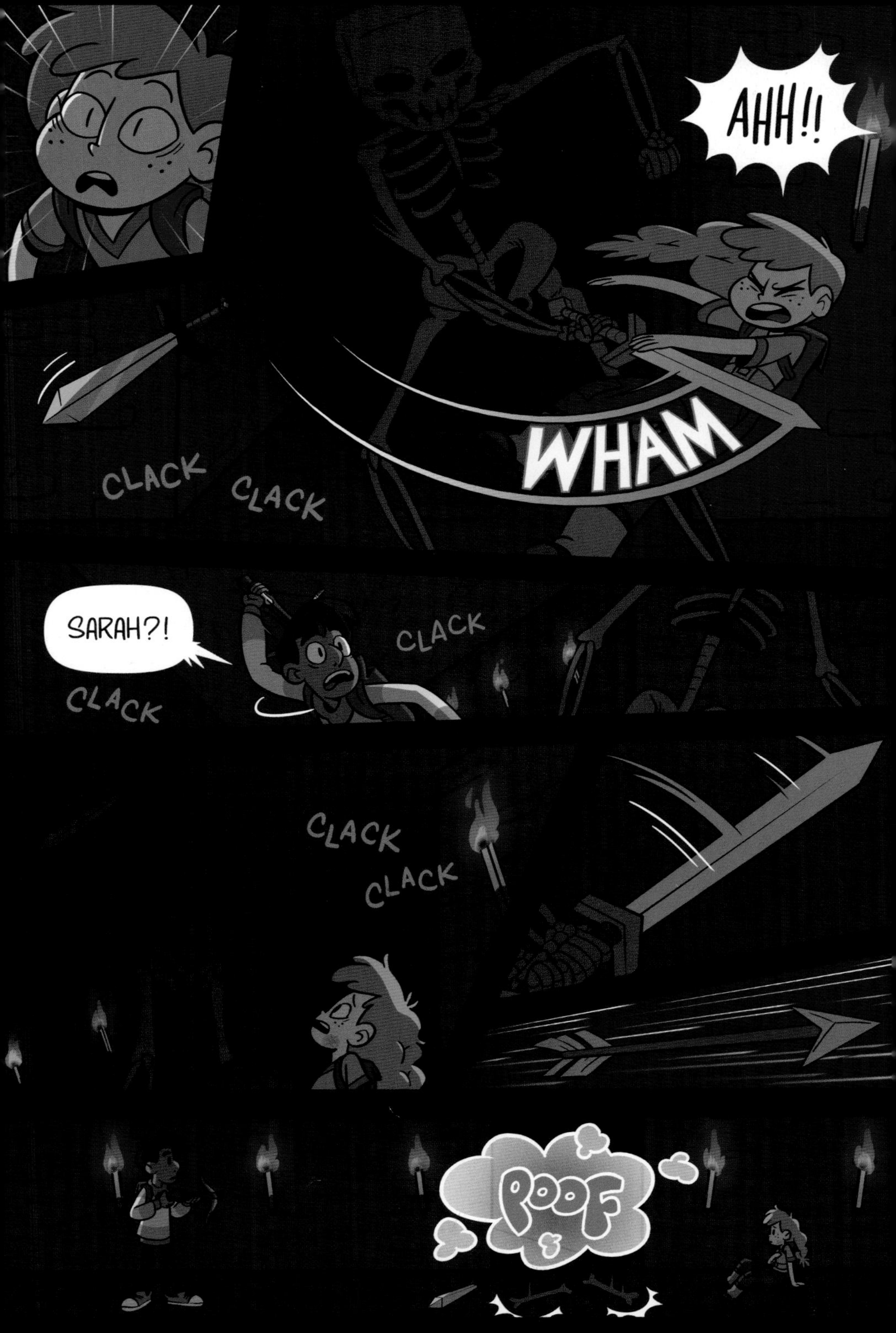

AHH!!
WHAM
CLACK
CLACK
SARAH?!
CLACK
CLACK
CLACK
CLACK
POOF

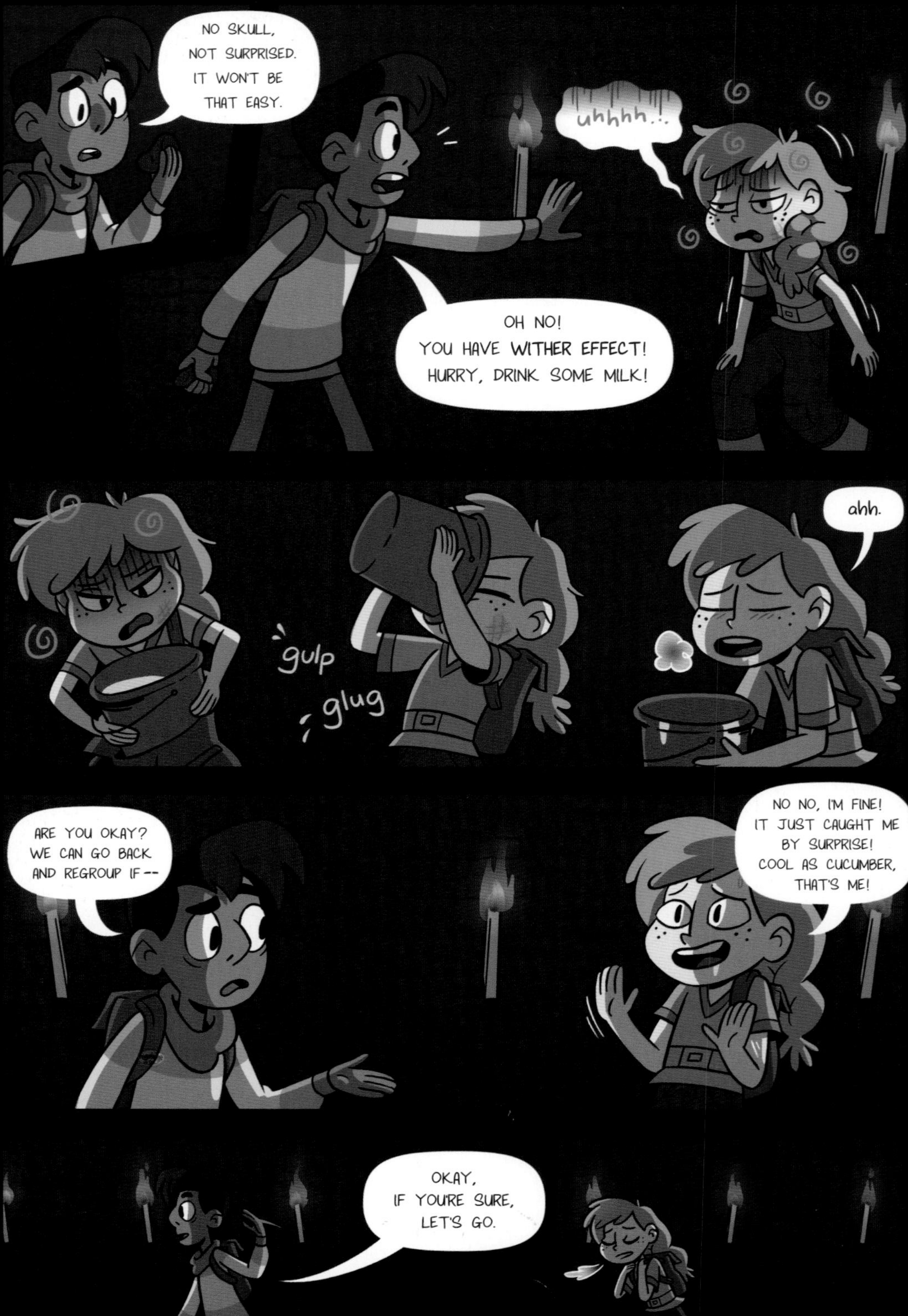
NO SKULL, NOT SURPRISED. IT WON'T BE THAT EASY.
uhhhh...
OH NO! YOU HAVE WITHER EFFECT! HURRY, DRINK SOME MILK!
gulp
glug
ahh.
ARE YOU OKAY? WE CAN GO BACK AND REGROUP IF--
NO NO, I'M FINE! IT JUST CAUGHT ME BY SURPRISE! COOL AS CUCUMBER, THAT'S ME!
OKAY, IF YOU'RE SURE, LET'S GO.

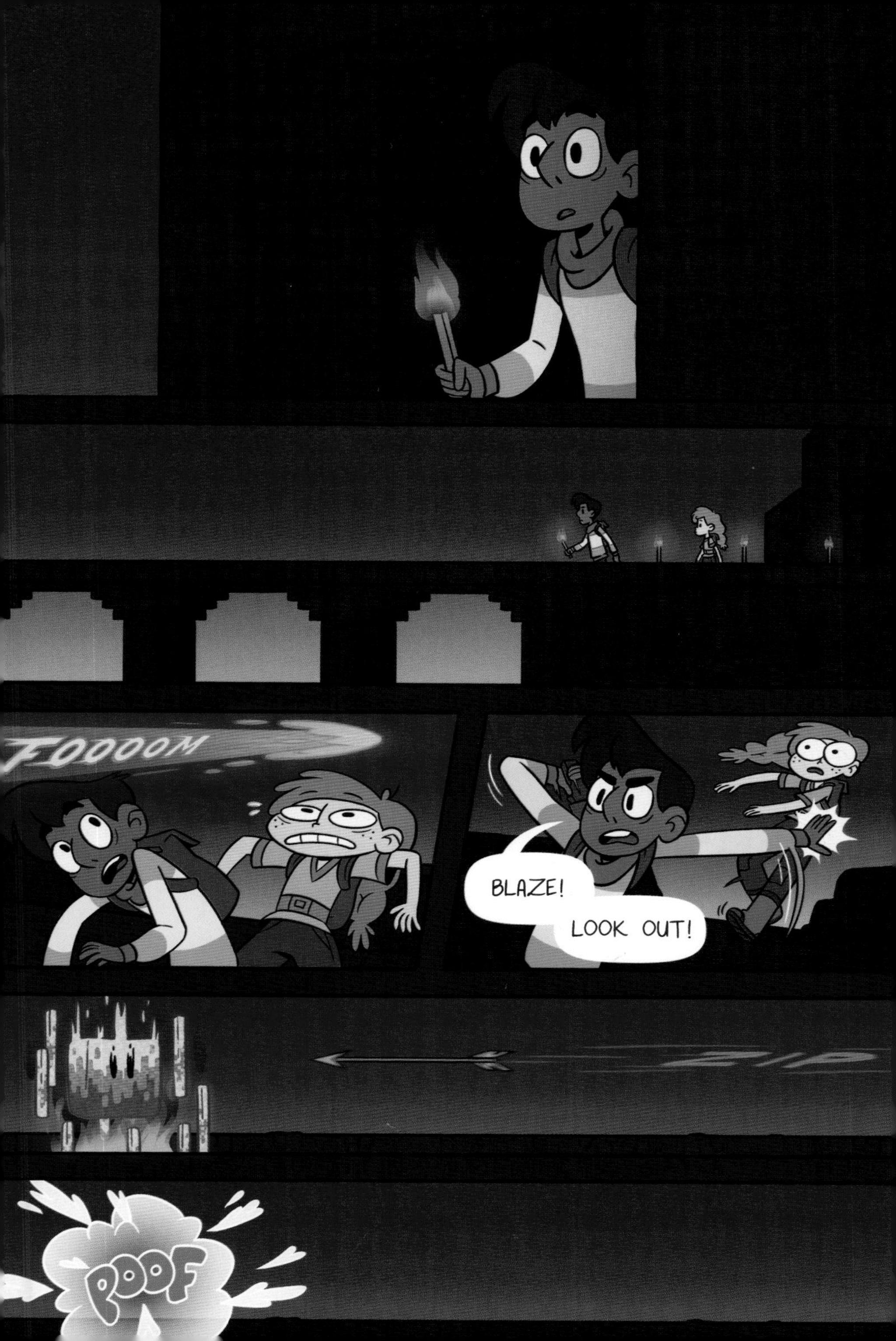
FOOOOM
BLAZE!
LOOK OUT!
ZIIP
POOF

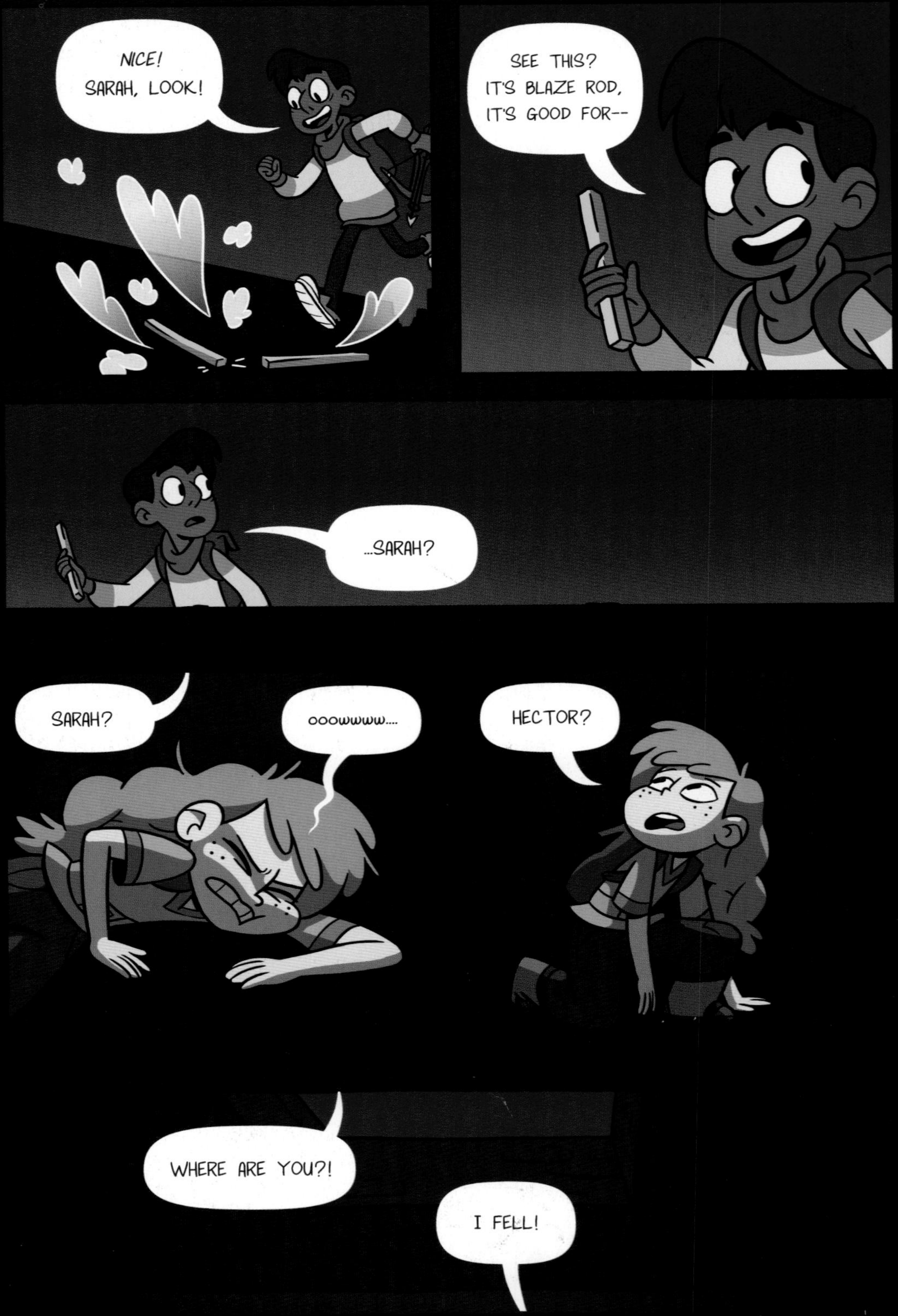
NICE!
SARAH, LOOK!
SEE THIS?
IT'S BLAZE ROD,
IT'S GOOD FOR--
...SARAH?
SARAH?
ooowwww....
HECTOR?
WHERE ARE YOU?!
I FELL!

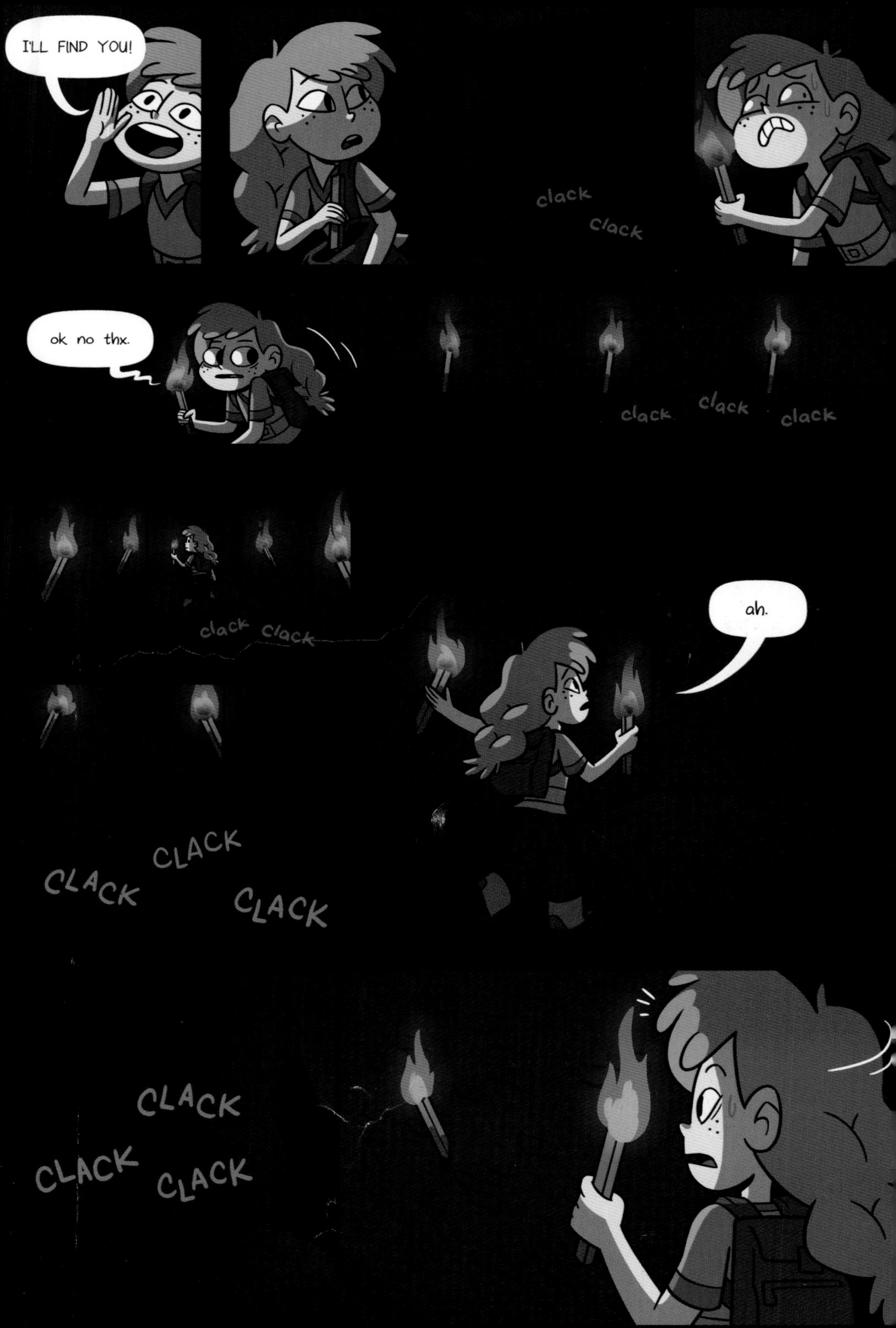
I'LL FIND YOU!
clack
clack
ok no thx.
clack
clack
clack
clack
clack
ah.
CLACK
CLACK
CLACK
CLACK
CLACK
CLACK

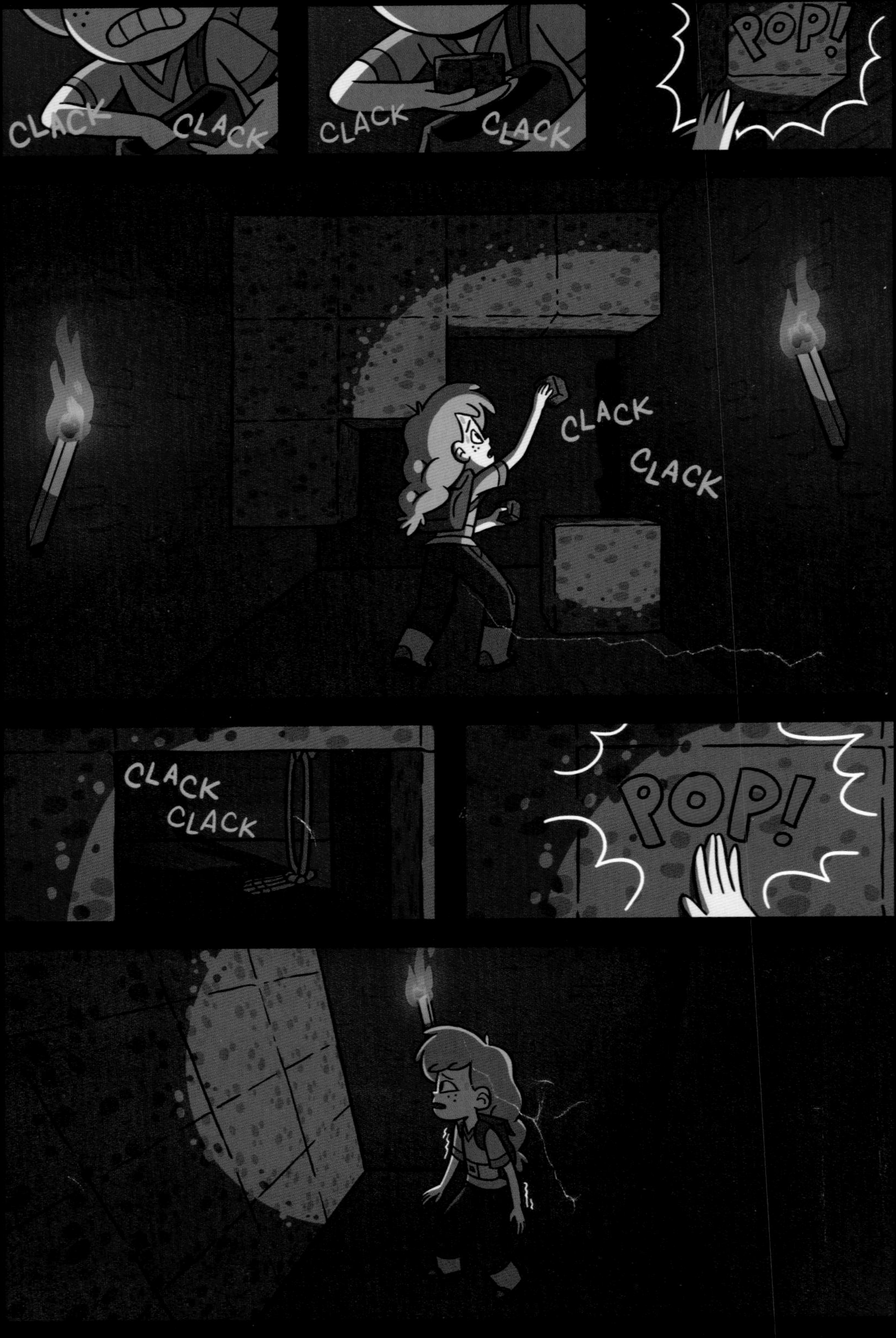
CLACK
CLACK
CLACK
CLACK
POP!
CLACK
CLACK
CLACK
CLACK
POP!

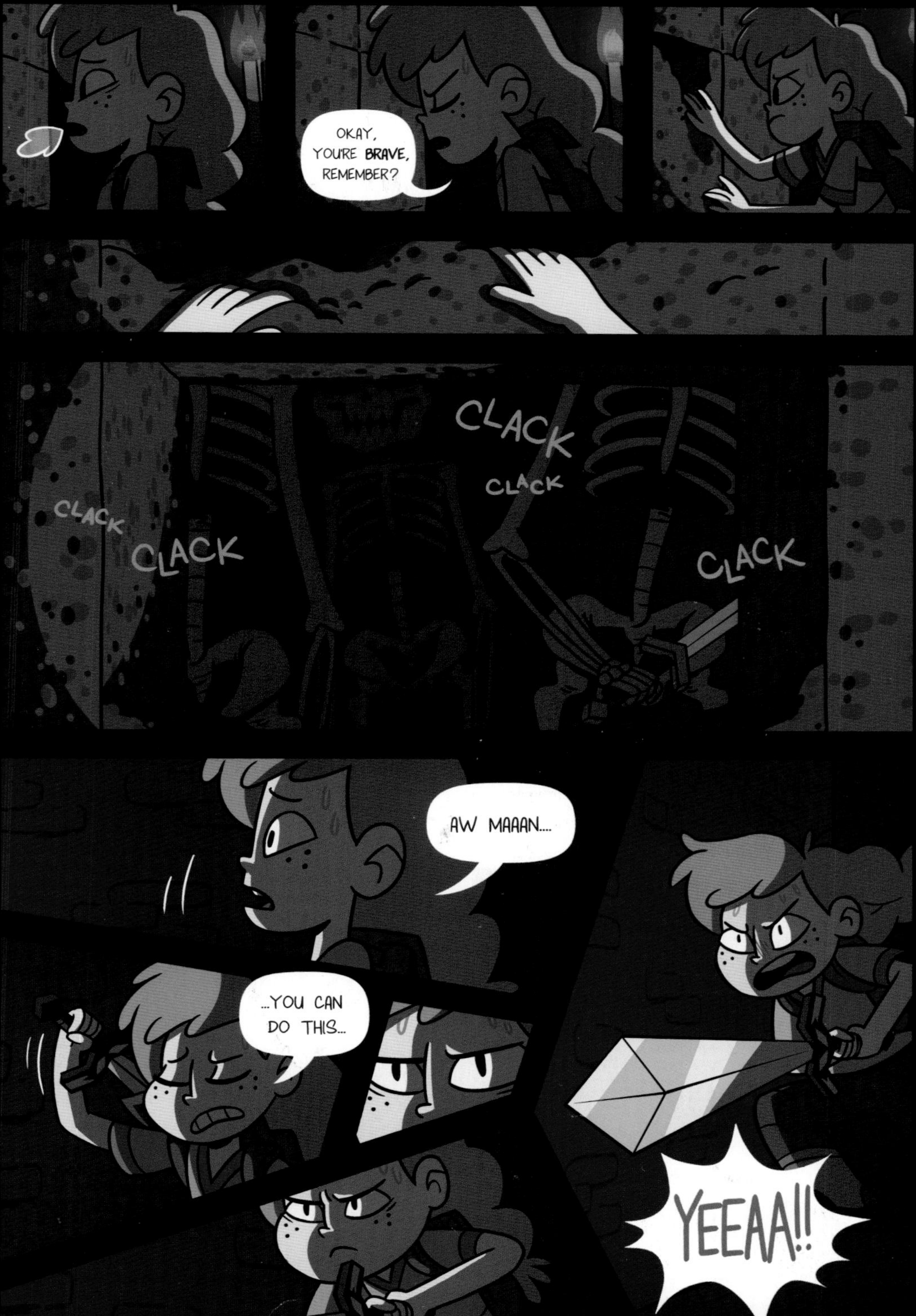
OKAY, YOU'RE BRAVE, REMEMBER?
CLACK
CLACK
CLACK
CLACK
CLACK
AW MAAAN....
...YOU CAN DO THIS...
YEEAA!!

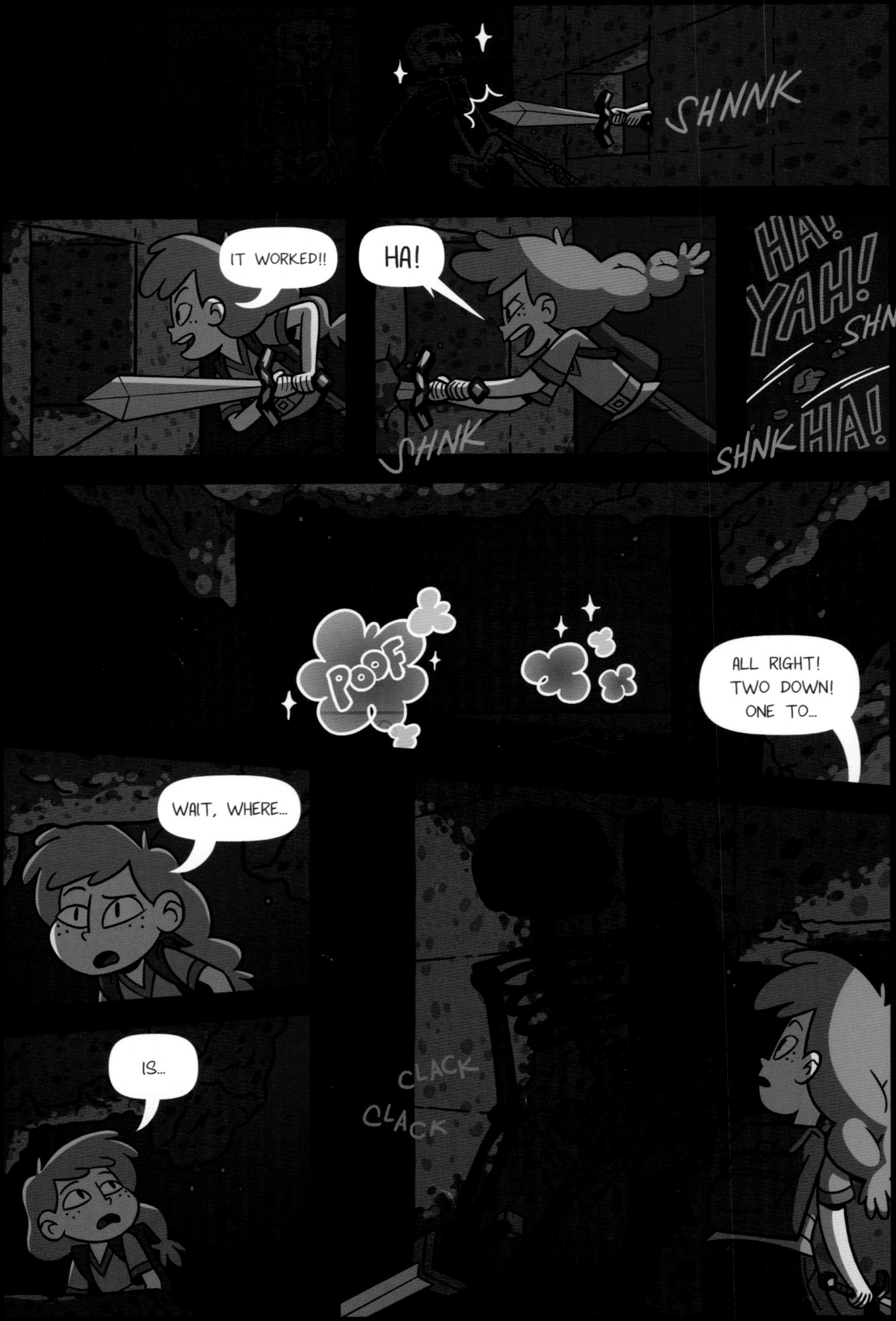
SHNNK
IT WORKED!!
HA!
SHNK
HA!
YAH!
SHNK
SHNK
HA!
POOF
ALL RIGHT! TWO DOWN! ONE TO...
WAIT, WHERE...
IS...
CLACK
CLACK

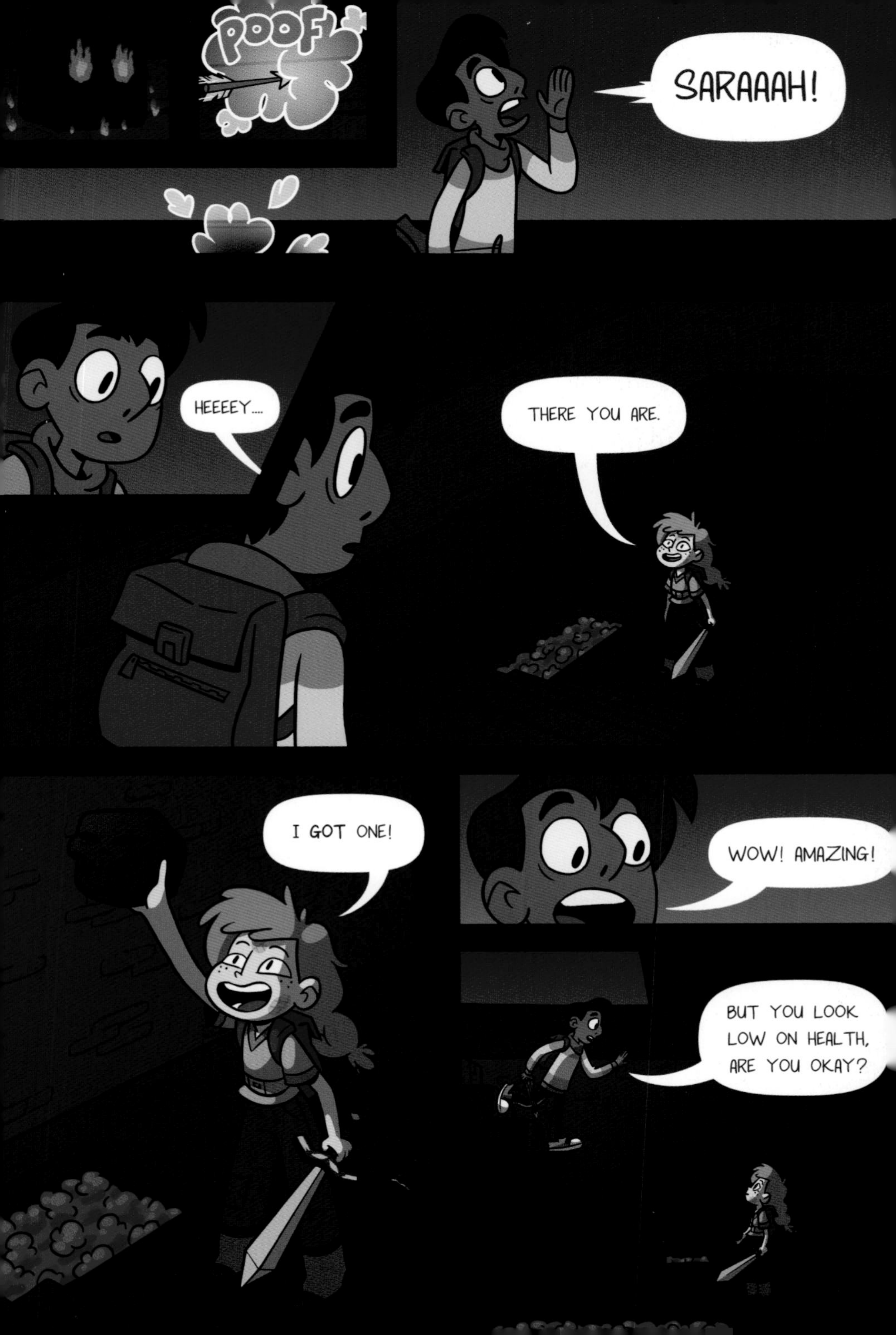
POOF
SARAAAH!
HEEEEY....
THERE YOU ARE.
I GOT ONE!
WOW! AMAZING!
BUT YOU LOOK LOW ON HEALTH, ARE YOU OKAY?

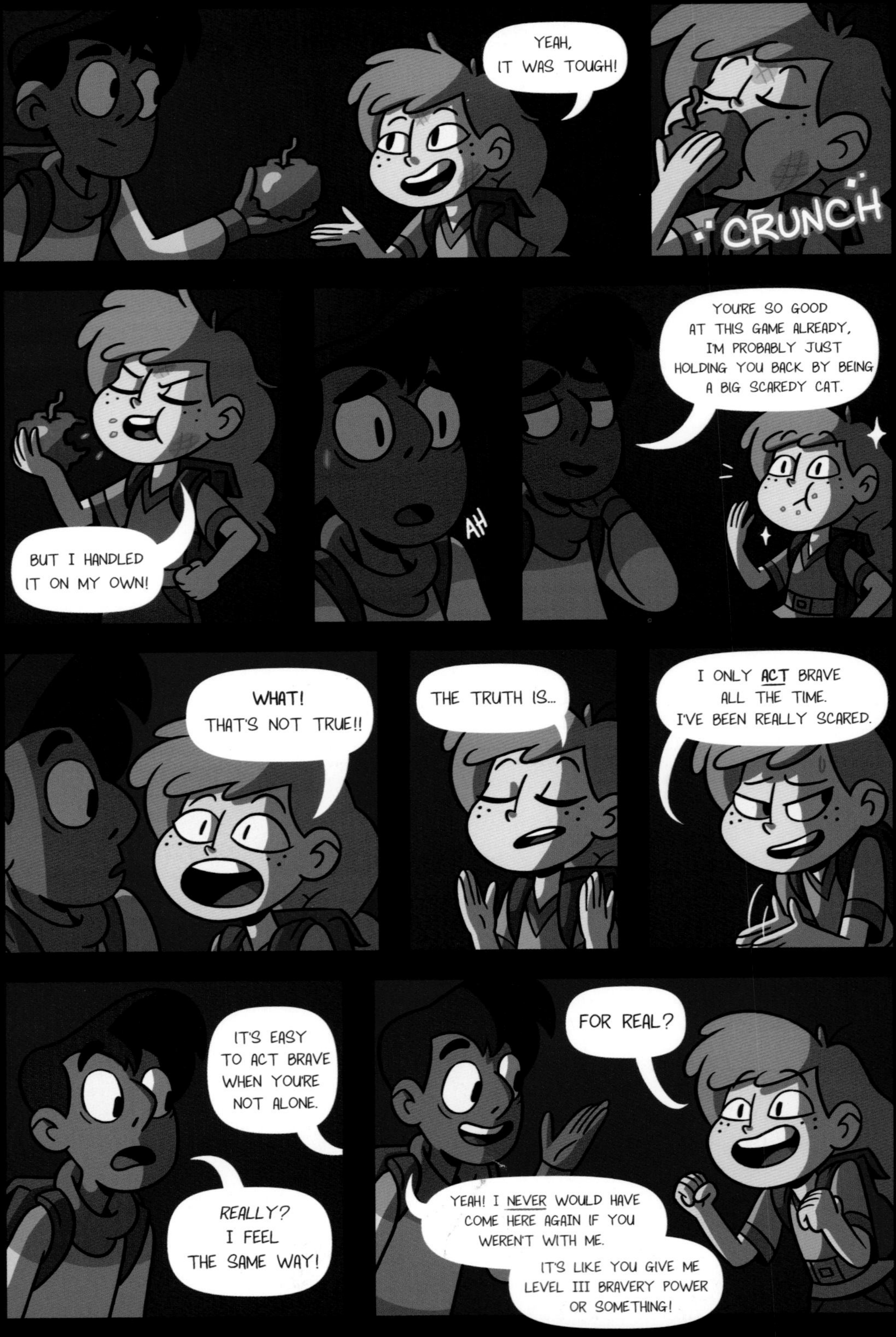
YEAH,
IT WAS TOUGH!
CRUNCH
BUT I HANDLED IT ON MY OWN!
AH
YOU'RE SO GOOD AT THIS GAME ALREADY, I'M PROBABLY JUST HOLDING YOU BACK BY BEING A BIG SCAREDY CAT.
WHAT! THAT'S NOT TRUE!!
THE TRUTH IS...
I ONLY ACT BRAVE ALL THE TIME. I'VE BEEN REALLY SCARED.
IT'S EASY TO ACT BRAVE WHEN YOU'RE NOT ALONE.
REALLY? I FEEL THE SAME WAY!
FOR REAL?
YEAH! I NEVER WOULD HAVE COME HERE AGAIN IF YOU WEREN'T WITH ME.
IT'S LIKE YOU GIVE ME LEVEL III BRAVERY POWER OR SOMETHING!

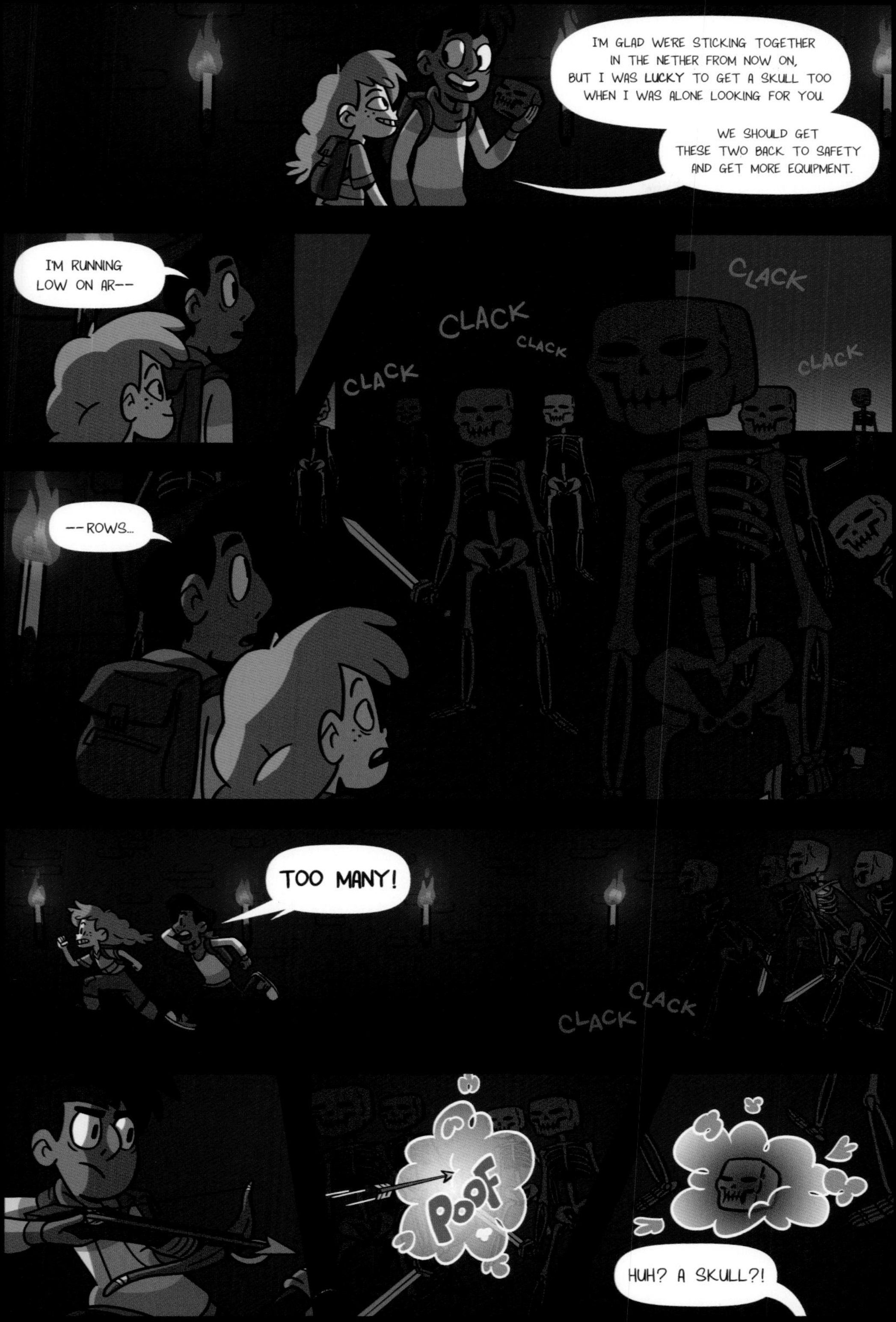
I'M GLAD WE'RE STICKING TOGETHER IN THE NETHER FROM NOW ON, BUT I WAS LUCKY TO GET A SKULL TOO WHEN I WAS ALONE LOOKING FOR YOU.
WE SHOULD GET THESE TWO BACK TO SAFETY AND GET MORE EQUIPMENT.
I'M RUNNING LOW ON AR--
CLACK
CLACK
CLACK
CLACK
CLACK
--ROWS...
TOO MANY!
CLACK
CLACK
POOF
HUH? A SKULL?!

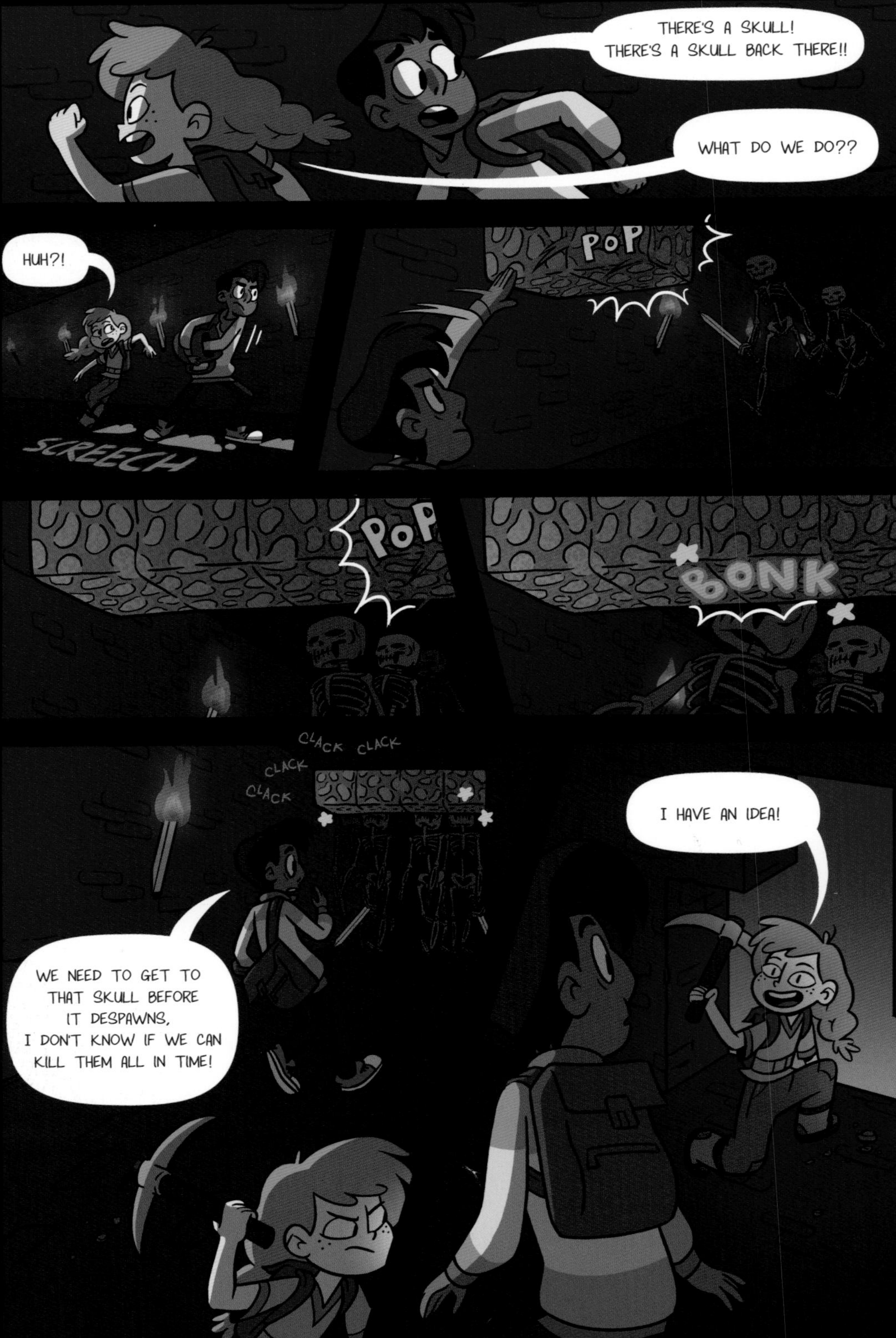
THERE'S A SKULL! THERE'S A SKULL BACK THERE!!
WHAT DO WE DO??
HUH?!
SCREEECH
POP
POP
BONK
CLACK
CLACK
CLACK CLACK
I HAVE AN IDEA!
WE NEED TO GET TO THAT SKULL BEFORE IT DESPAWNS, I DON'T KNOW IF WE CAN KILL THEM ALL IN TIME!

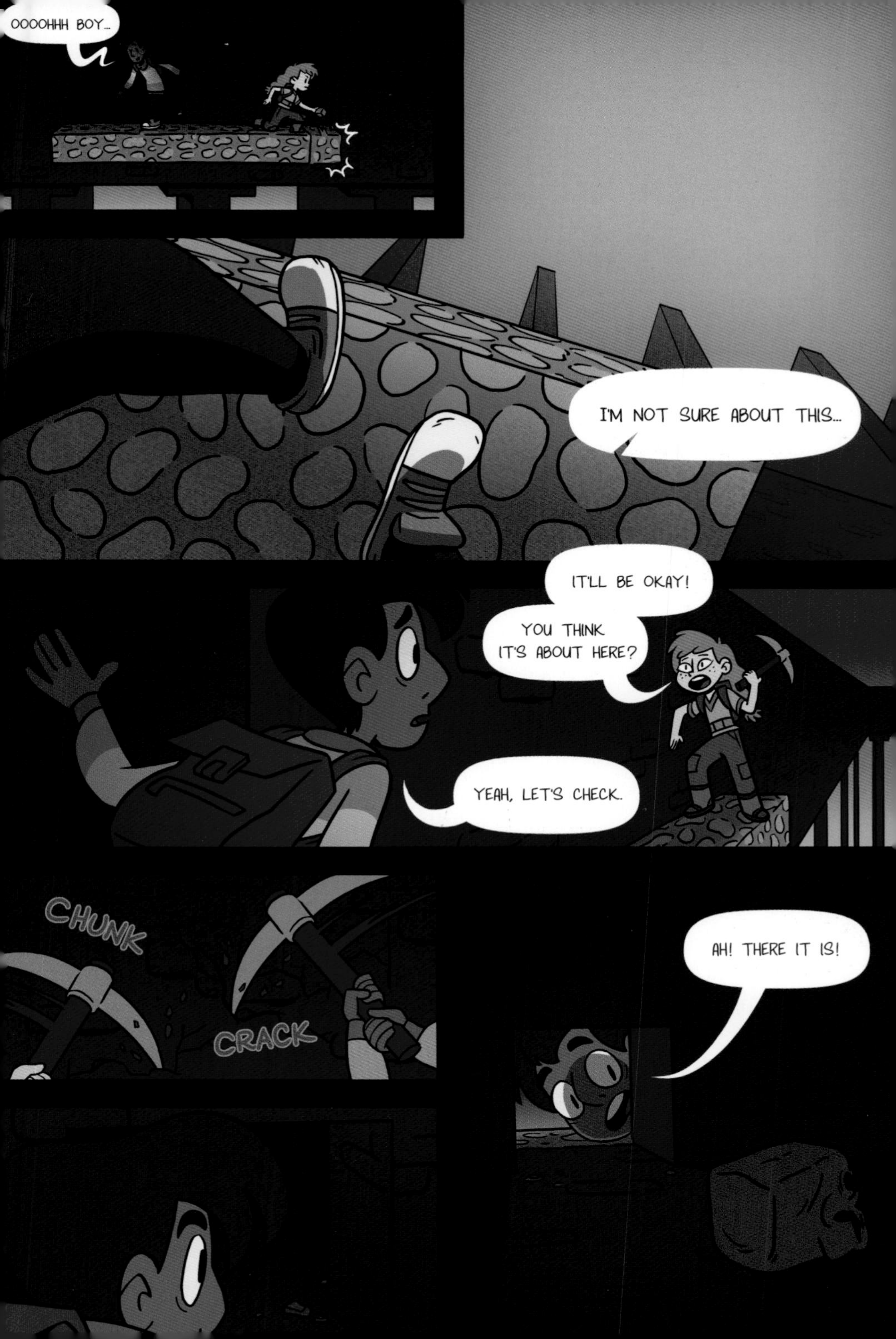
OOOOHHH BOY...
I'M NOT SURE ABOUT THIS...
IT'LL BE OKAY!
YOU THINK IT'S ABOUT HERE?
YEAH, LET'S CHECK.
CHUNK
CRACK
AH! THERE IT IS!

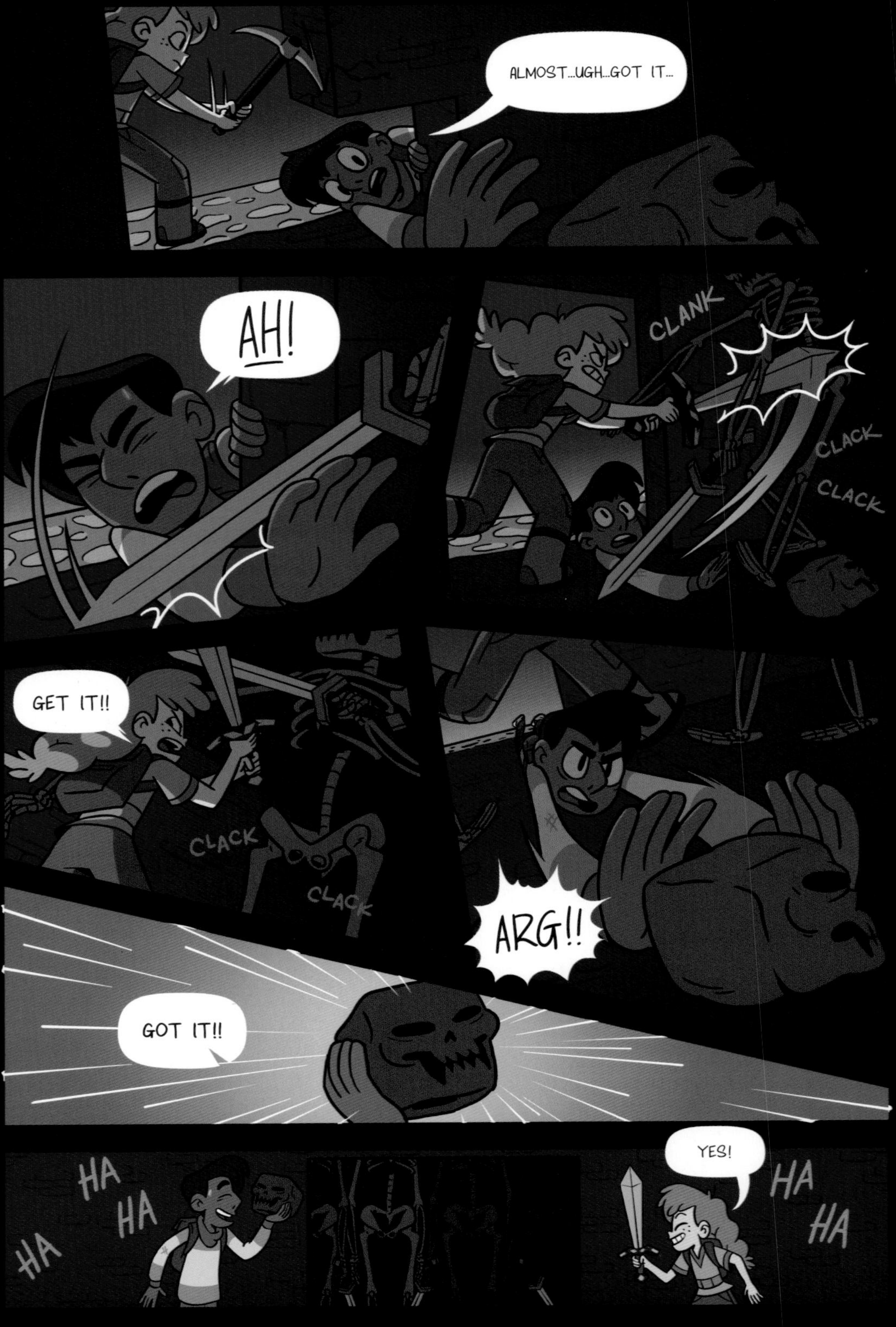
ALMOST...UGH...GOT IT...
AH!
CLANK
CLACK
CLACK
GET IT!!
CLACK
CLACK
ARG!!
GOT IT!!
HA
HA
HA
YES!
HA
HA

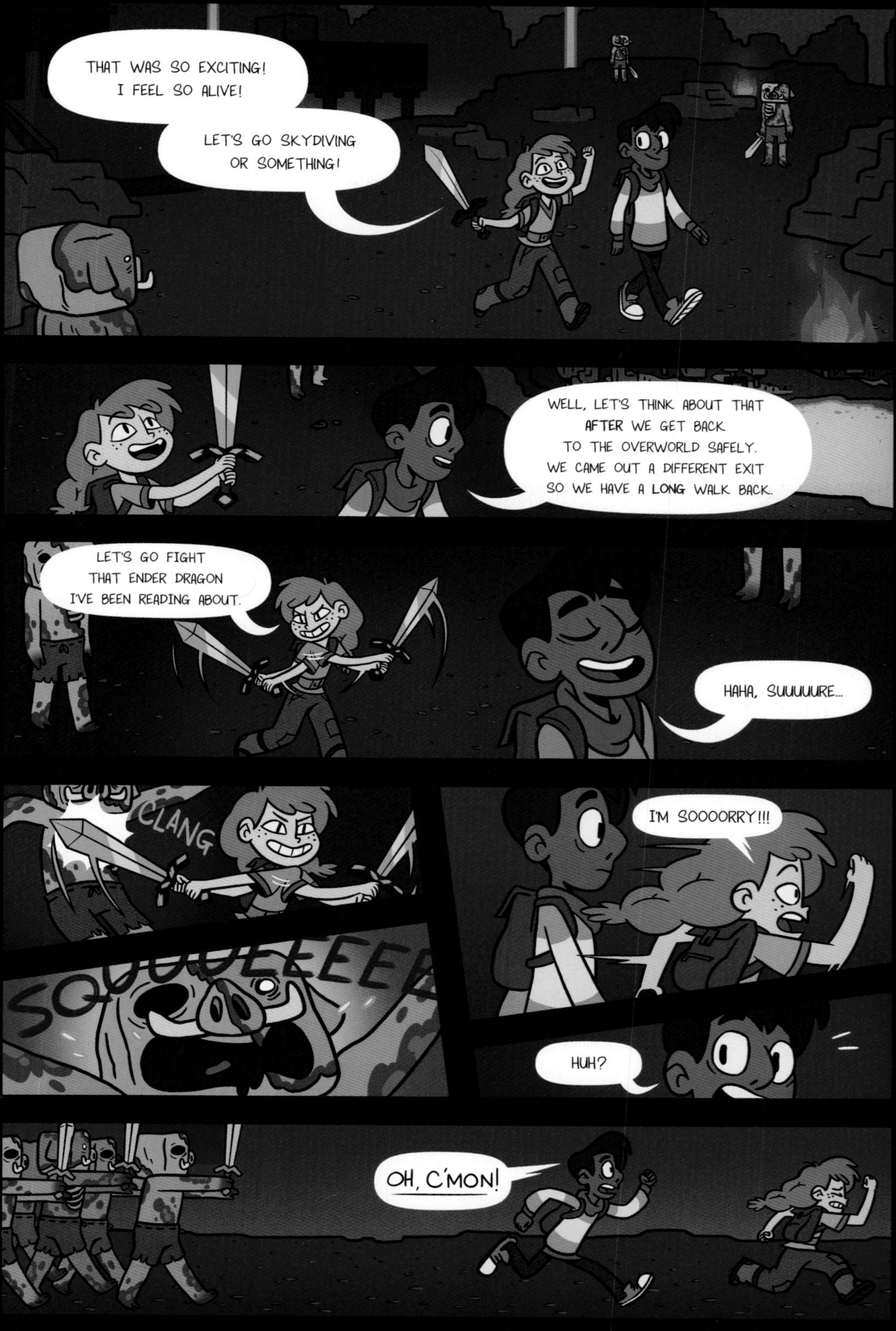
THAT WAS SO EXCITING! I FEEL SO ALIVE!
LET'S GO SKYDIVING OR SOMETHING!
WELL, LET'S THINK ABOUT THAT AFTER WE GET BACK TO THE OVERWORLD SAFELY. WE CAME OUT A DIFFERENT EXIT SO WE HAVE A LONG WALK BACK.
LET'S GO FIGHT THAT ENDER DRAGON I'VE BEEN READING ABOUT.
HAHA, SUUUUURE...
CLANG
SQUEEEE
I'M SOOOORRY!!!
HUH?
OH, C'MON!

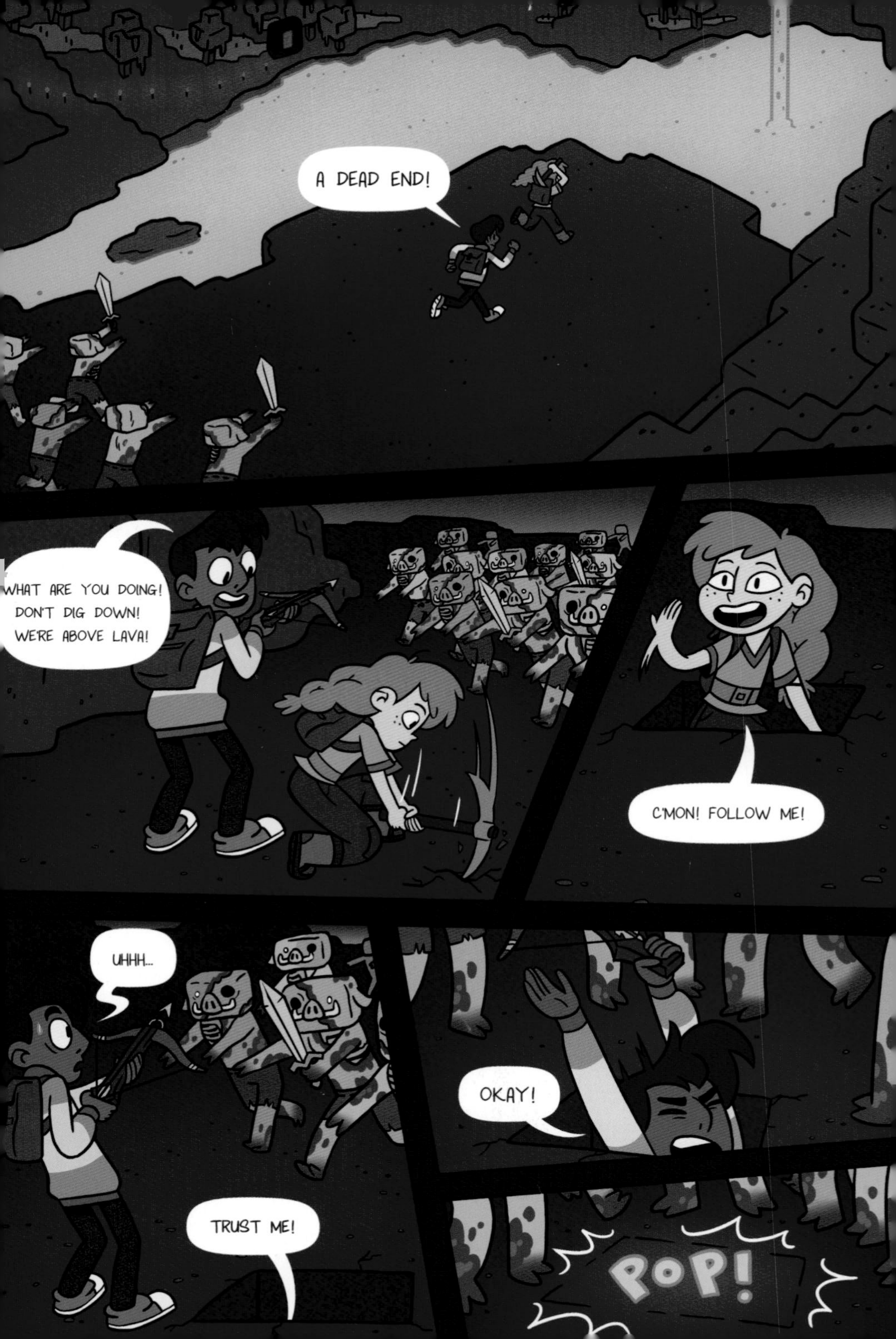

A DEAD END!
WHAT ARE YOU DOING! DON'T DIG DOWN! WE'RE ABOVE LAVA!
C'MON! FOLLOW ME!
UHHH...
TRUST ME!
OKAY!
POP!

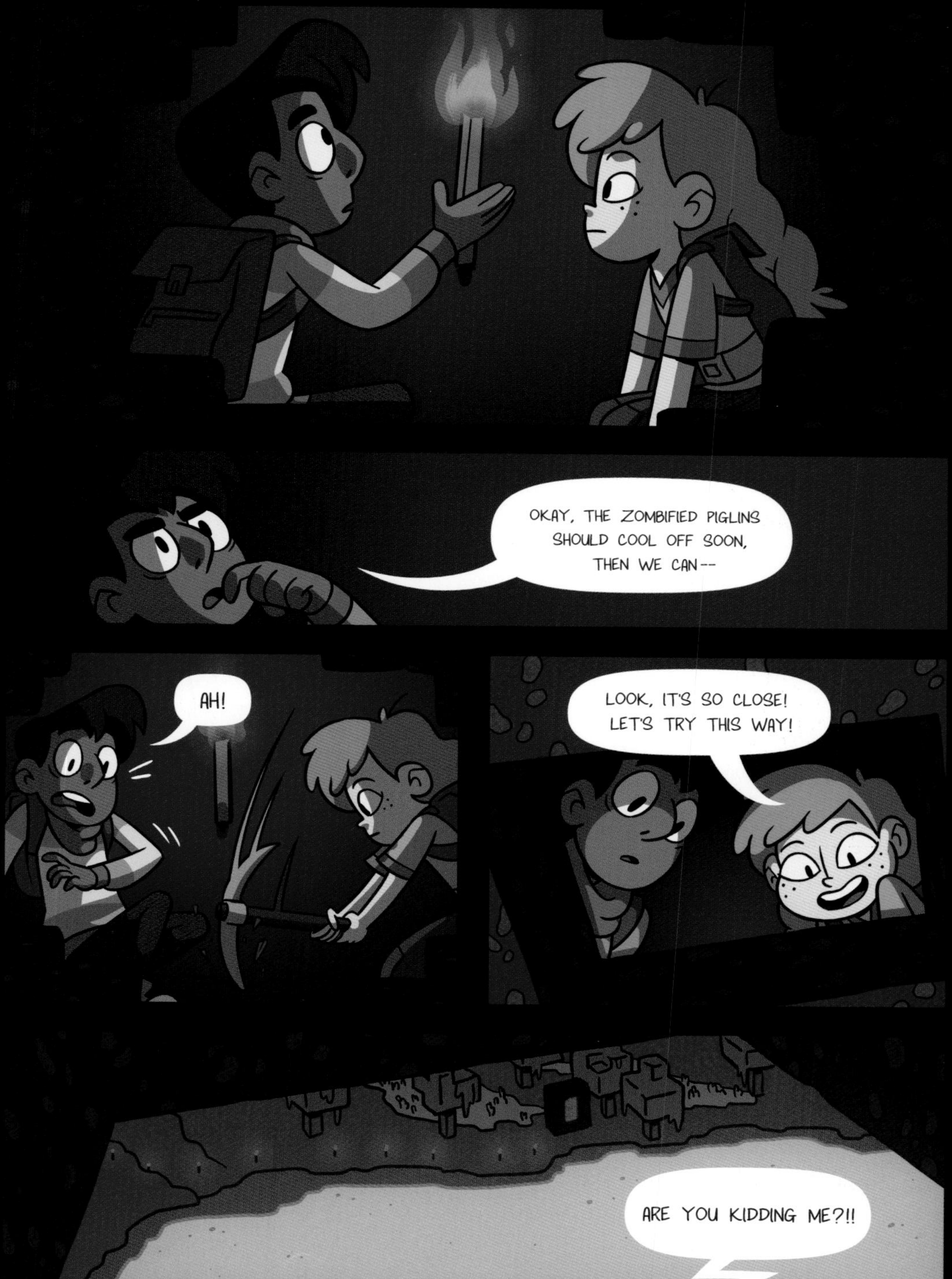
OKAY, THE ZOMBIFIED PIGLINS SHOULD COOL OFF SOON, THEN WE CAN--
AH!
LOOK, IT'S SO CLOSE! LET'S TRY THIS WAY!
ARE YOU KIDDING ME?!!

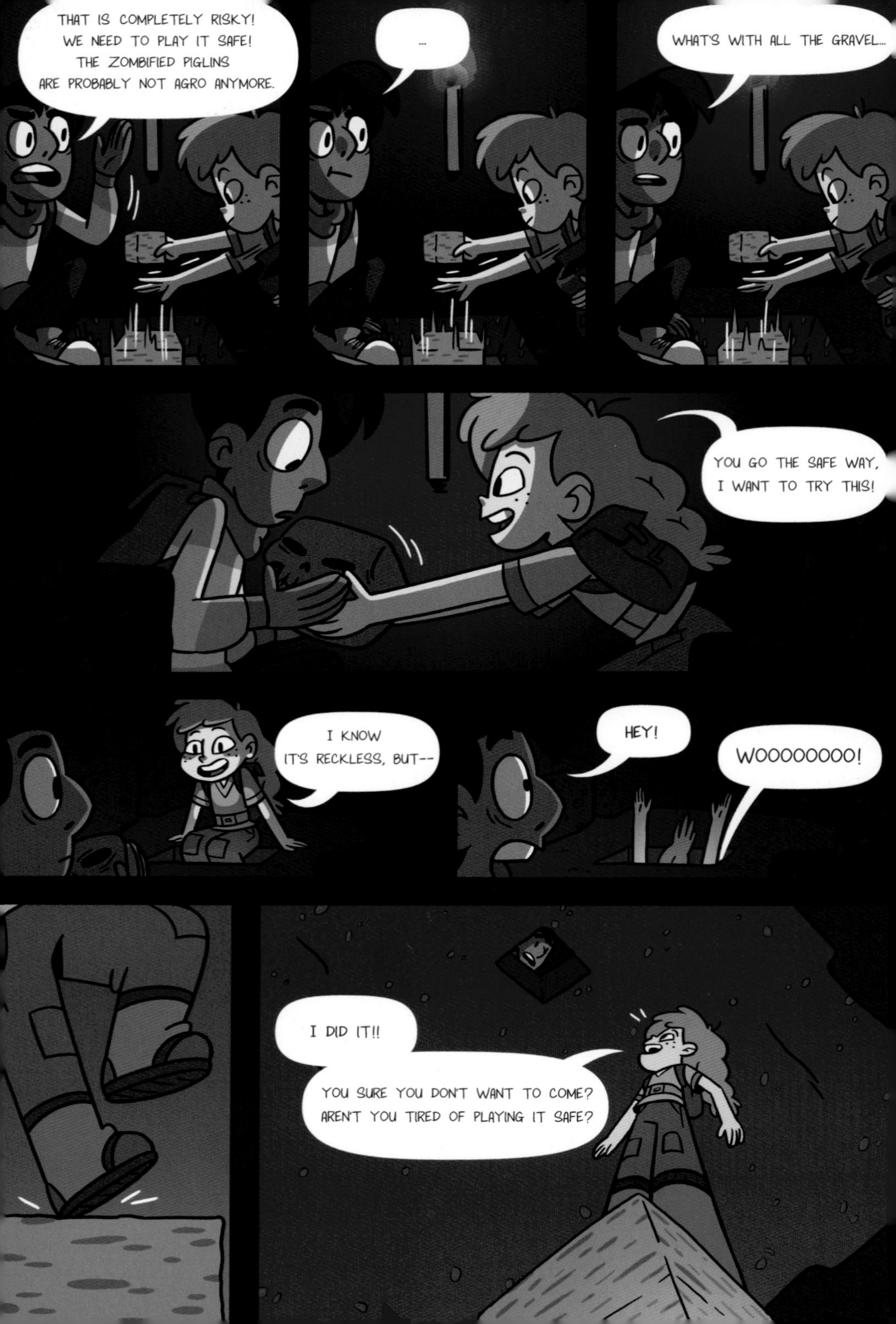
THAT IS COMPLETELY RISKY! WE NEED TO PLAY IT SAFE! THE ZOMBIFIED PIGLINS ARE PROBABLY NOT AGRO ANYMORE.
...
WHAT'S WITH ALL THE GRAVEL...
YOU GO THE SAFE WAY, I WANT TO TRY THIS!
I KNOW IT'S RECKLESS, BUT--
HEY!
WOOOOOOOO!
I DID IT!!
YOU SURE YOU DON'T WANT TO COME? AREN'T YOU TIRED OF PLAYING IT SAFE?

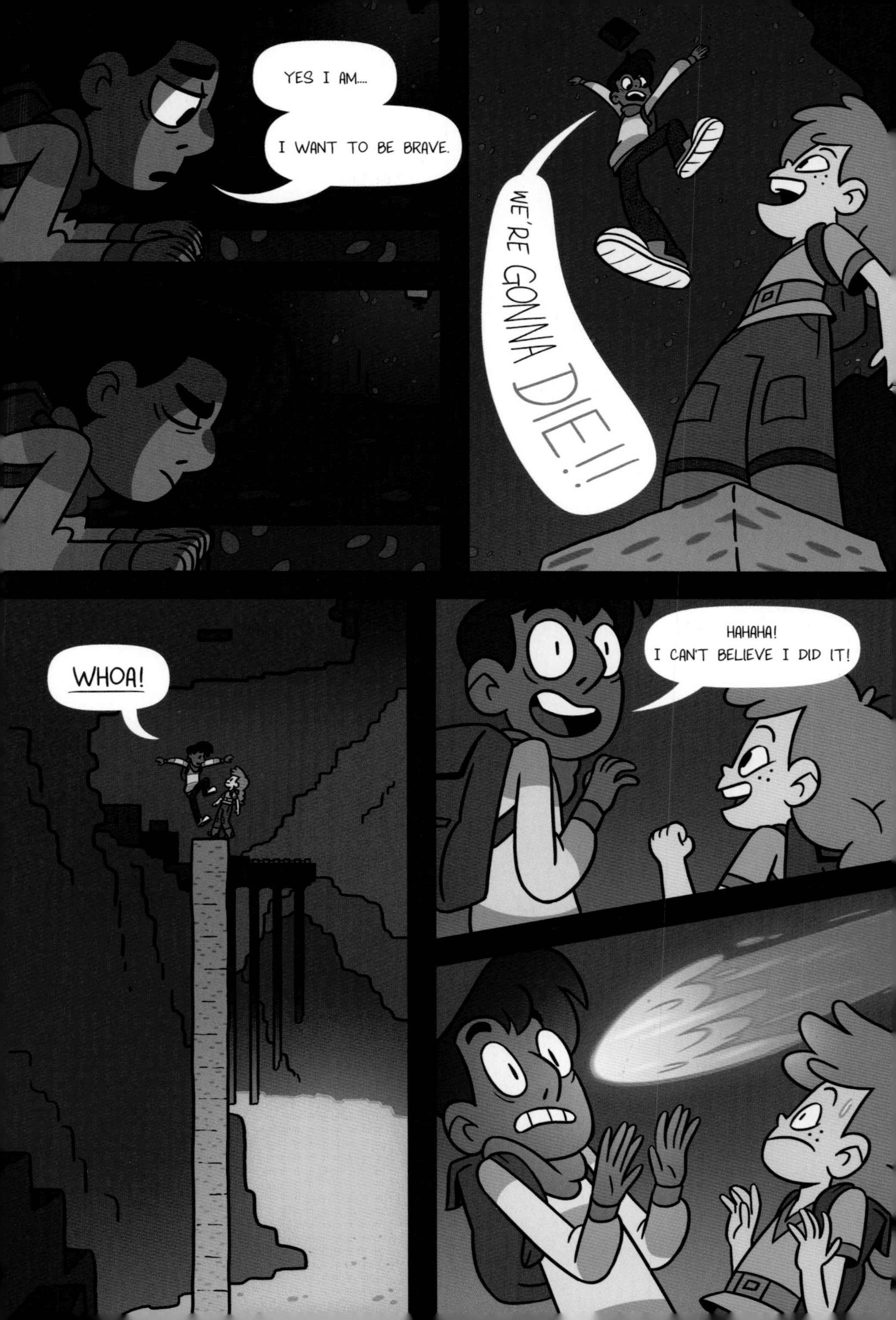

YES I AM....
I WANT TO BE BRAVE.
WE'RE GONNA DIE!!
WHOA!
HAHAHA! I CAN'T BELIEVE I DID IT!

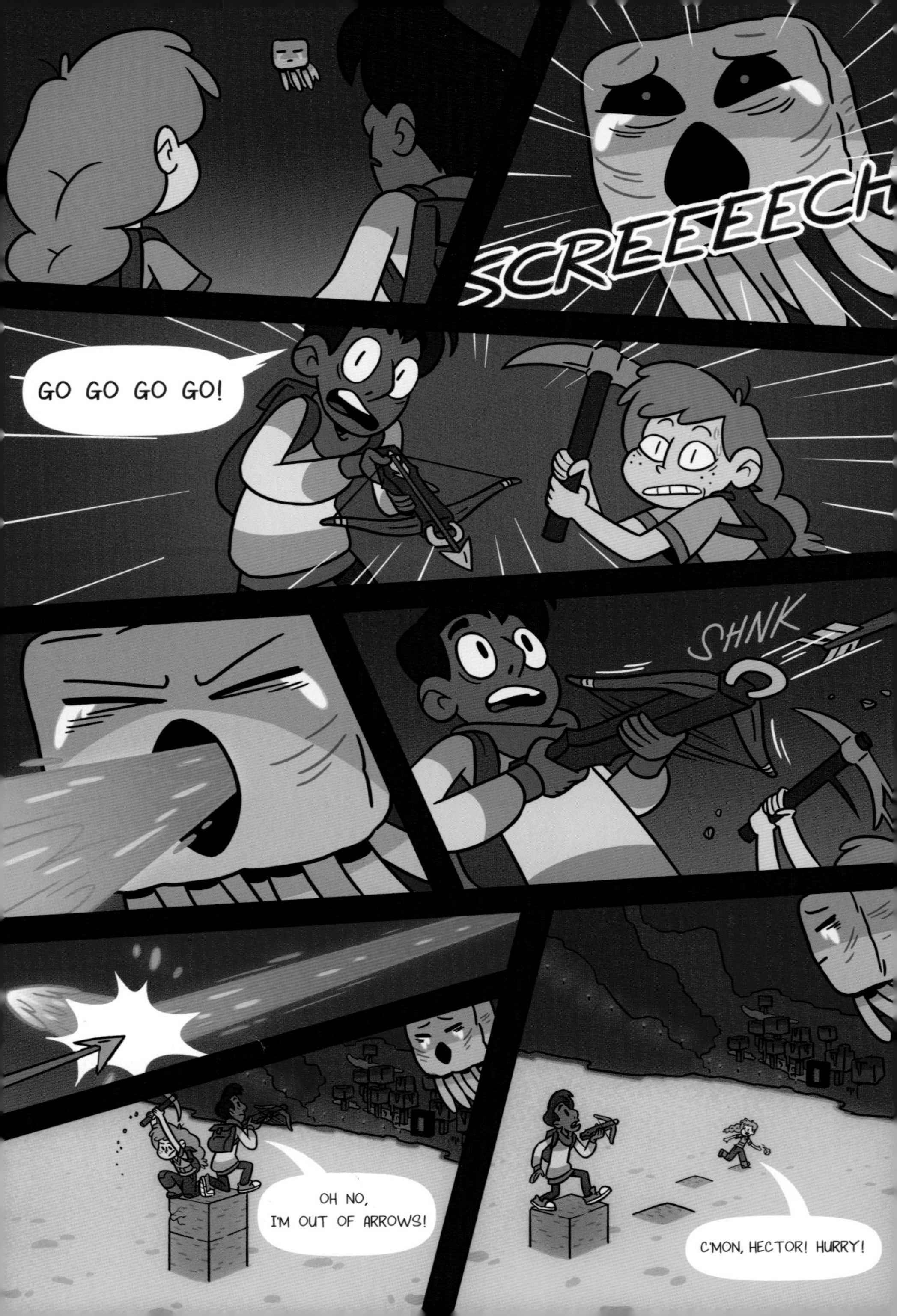
SCREEEEECH
GO GO GO GO!
SHNK
OH NO, I'M OUT OF ARROWS!
C'MON, HECTOR! HURRY!

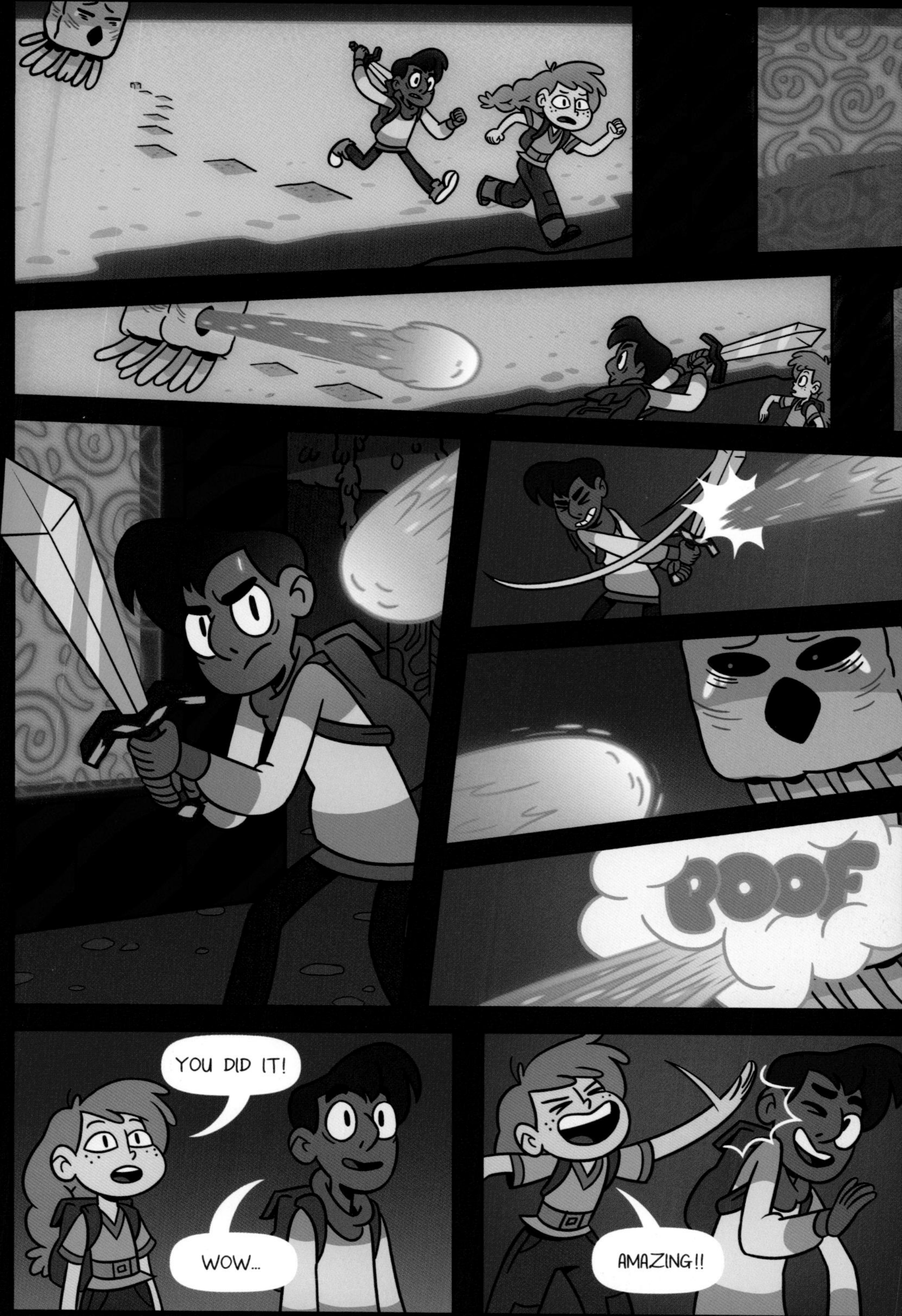
POOF
YOU DID IT!
WOW...
AMAZING!!

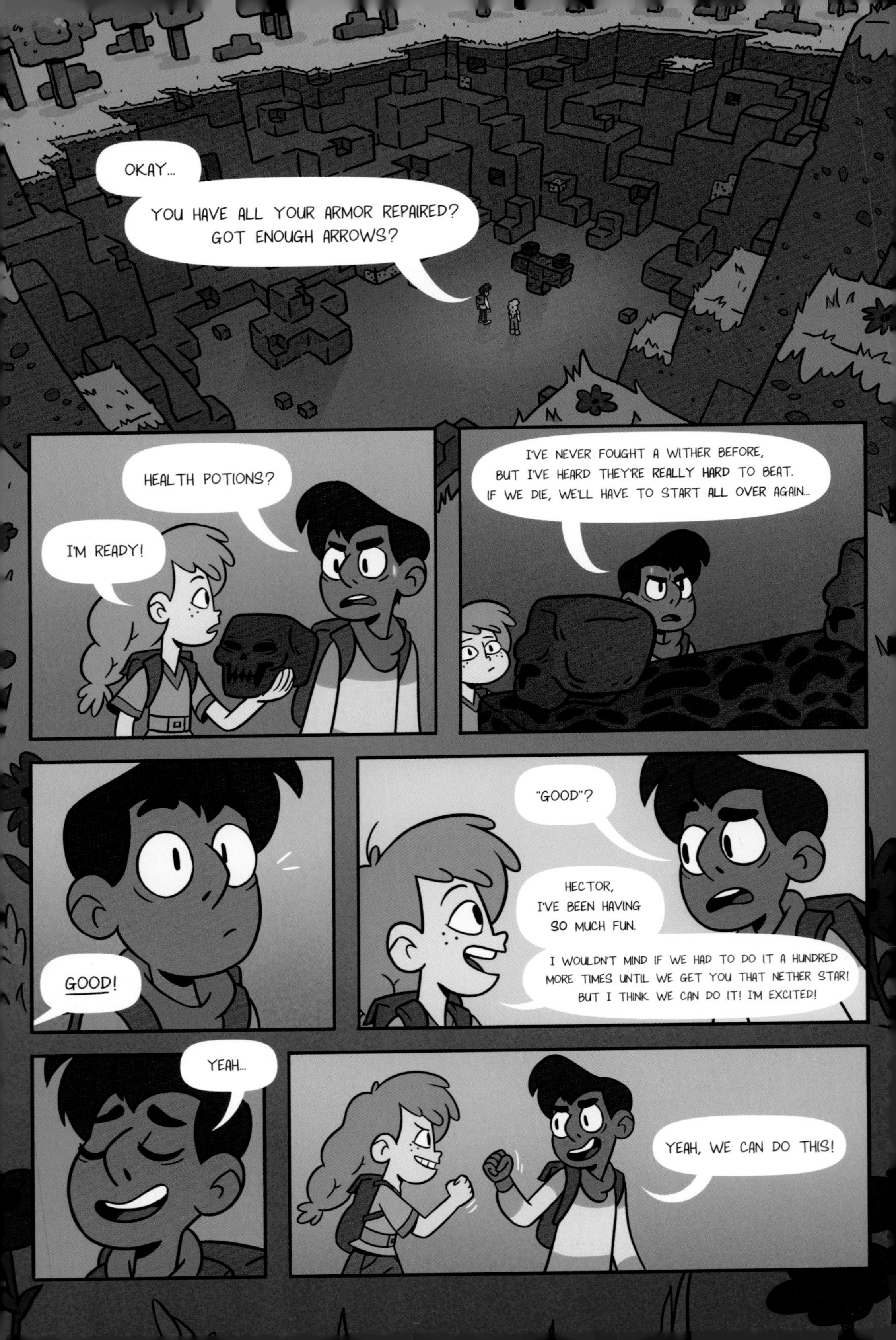
OKAY...
YOU HAVE ALL YOUR ARMOR REPAIRED? GOT ENOUGH ARROWS?
HEALTH POTIONS?
I'M READY!
I'VE NEVER FOUGHT A WITHER BEFORE, BUT I'VE HEARD THEY'RE REALLY HARD TO BEAT. IF WE DIE, WE'LL HAVE TO START ALL OVER AGAIN...
GOOD!
"GOOD"?
HECTOR, I'VE BEEN HAVING SO MUCH FUN.
I WOULDN'T MIND IF WE HAD TO DO IT A HUNDRED MORE TIMES UNTIL WE GET YOU THAT NETHER STAR! BUT I THINK WE CAN DO IT! I'M EXCITED!
YEAH...
YEAH, WE CAN DO THIS!

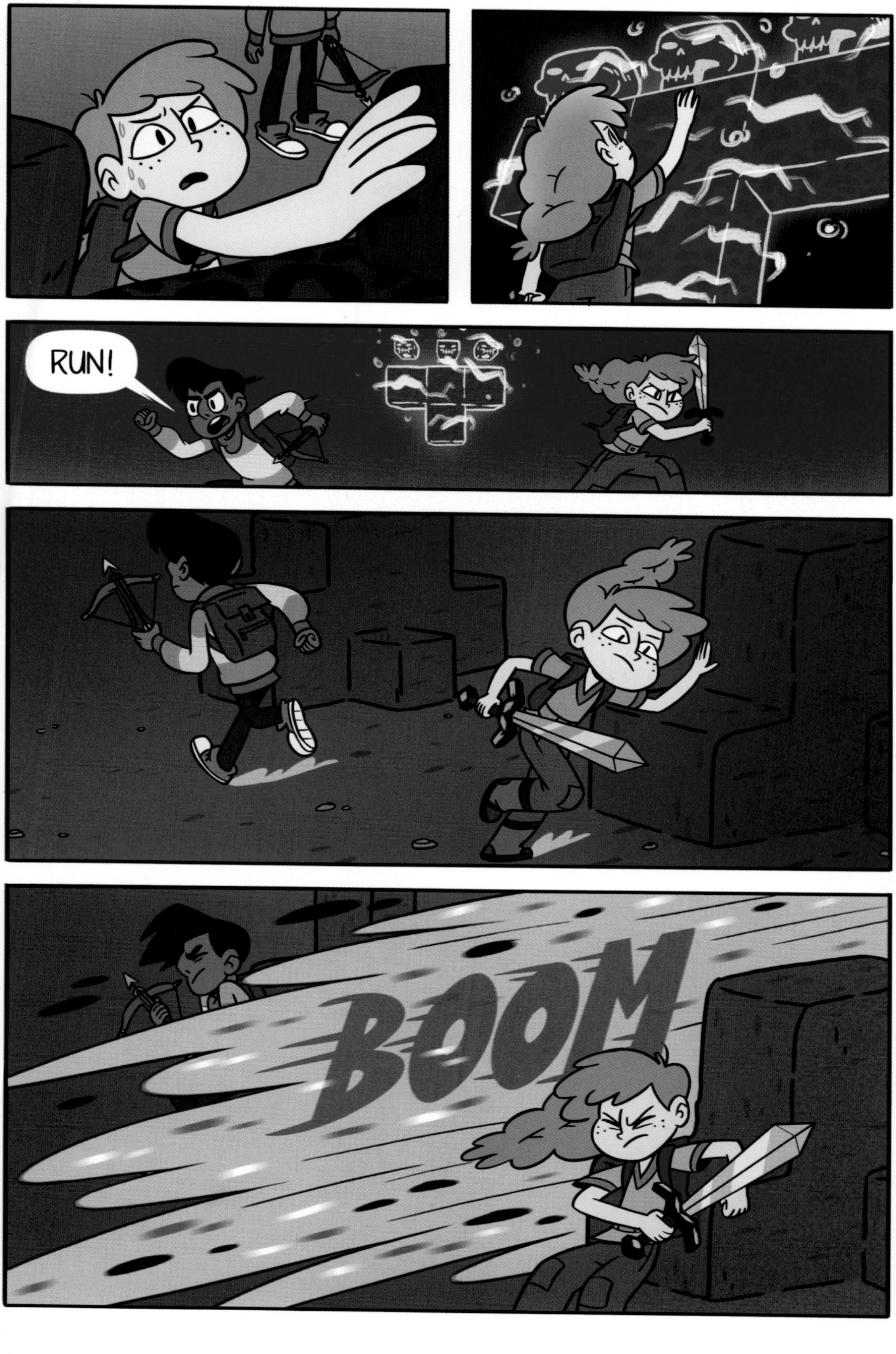
RUN!
BOOM

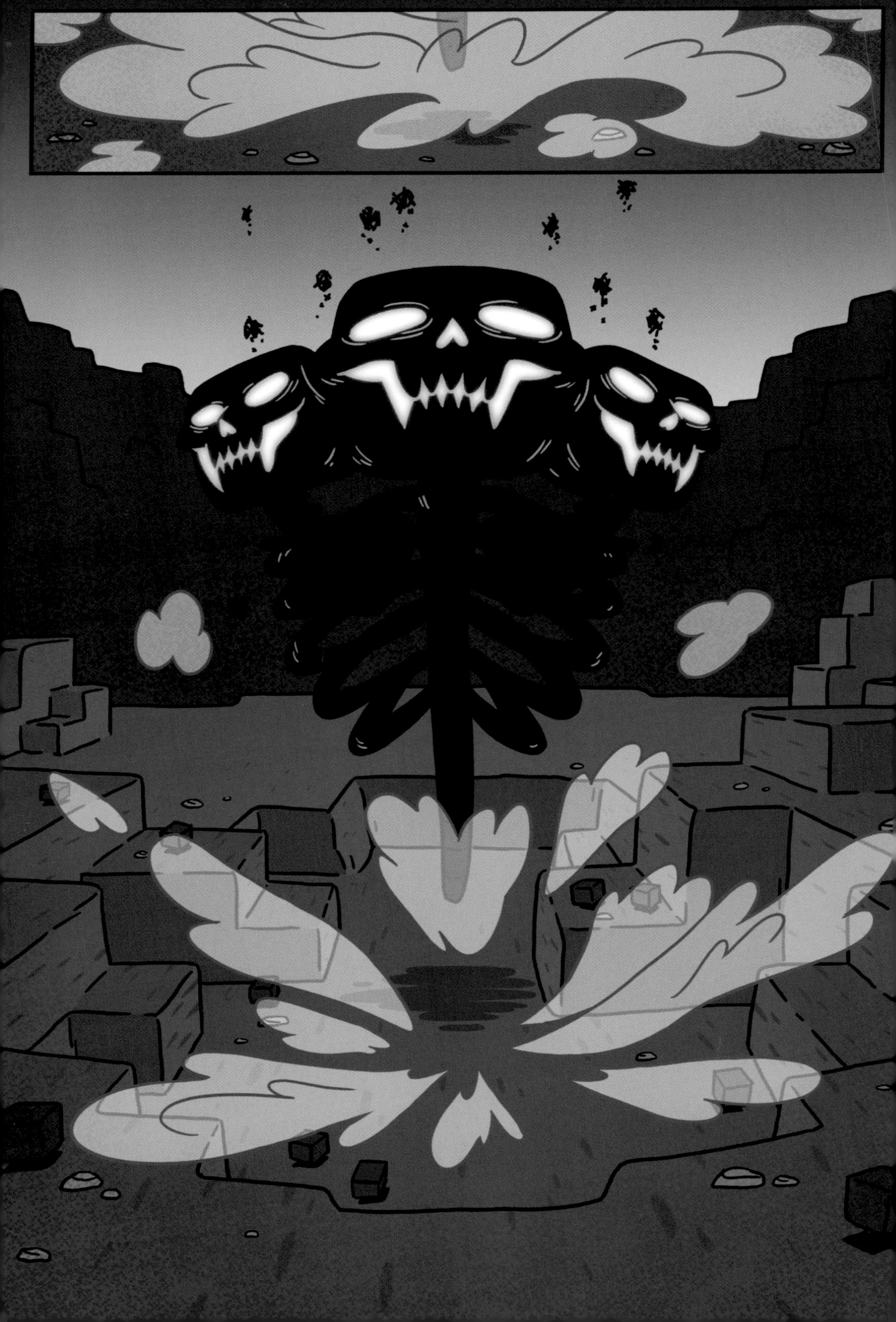

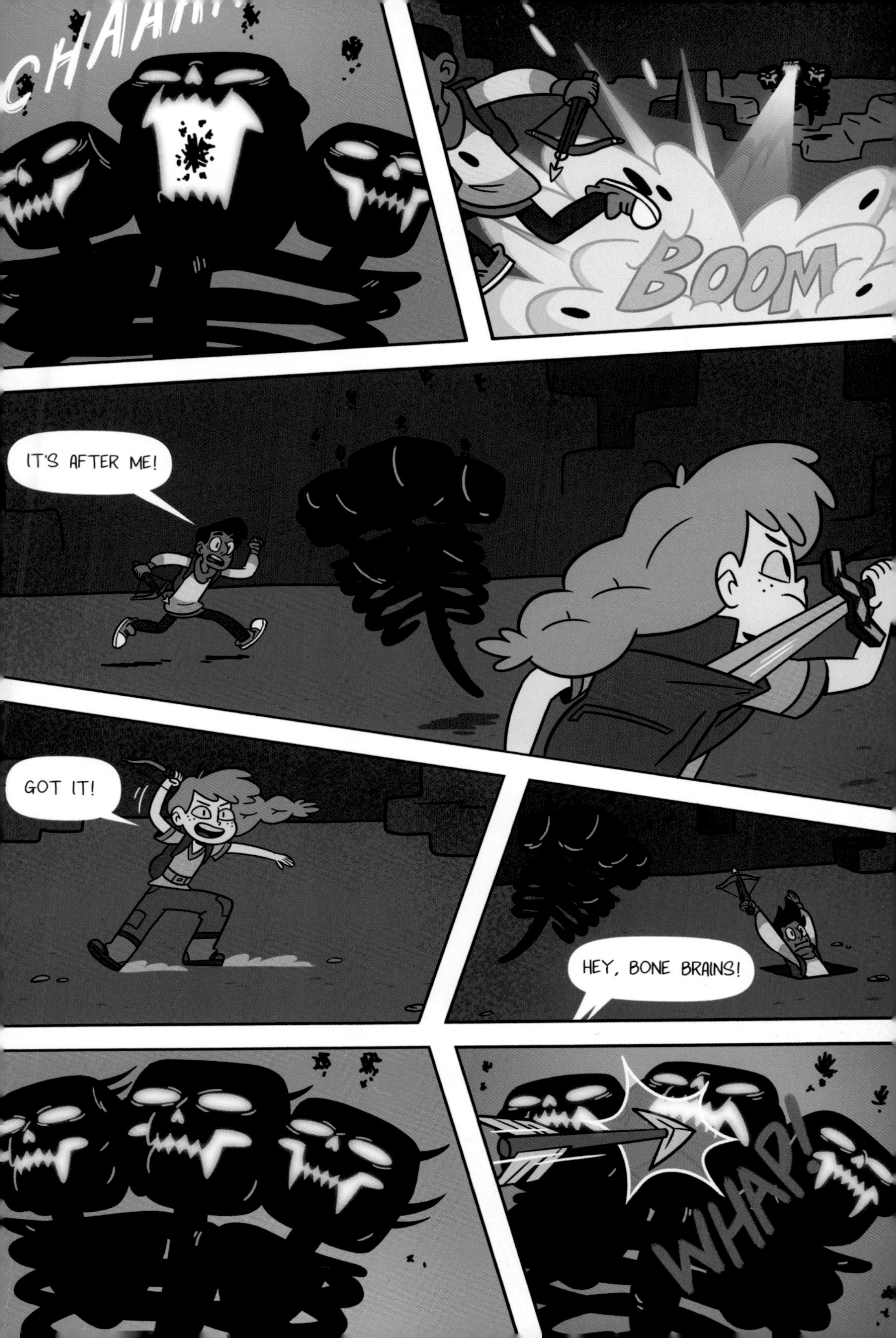
CHAAAH!
BOOM
IT'S AFTER ME!
GOT IT!
HEY, BONE BRAINS!
WHAP!

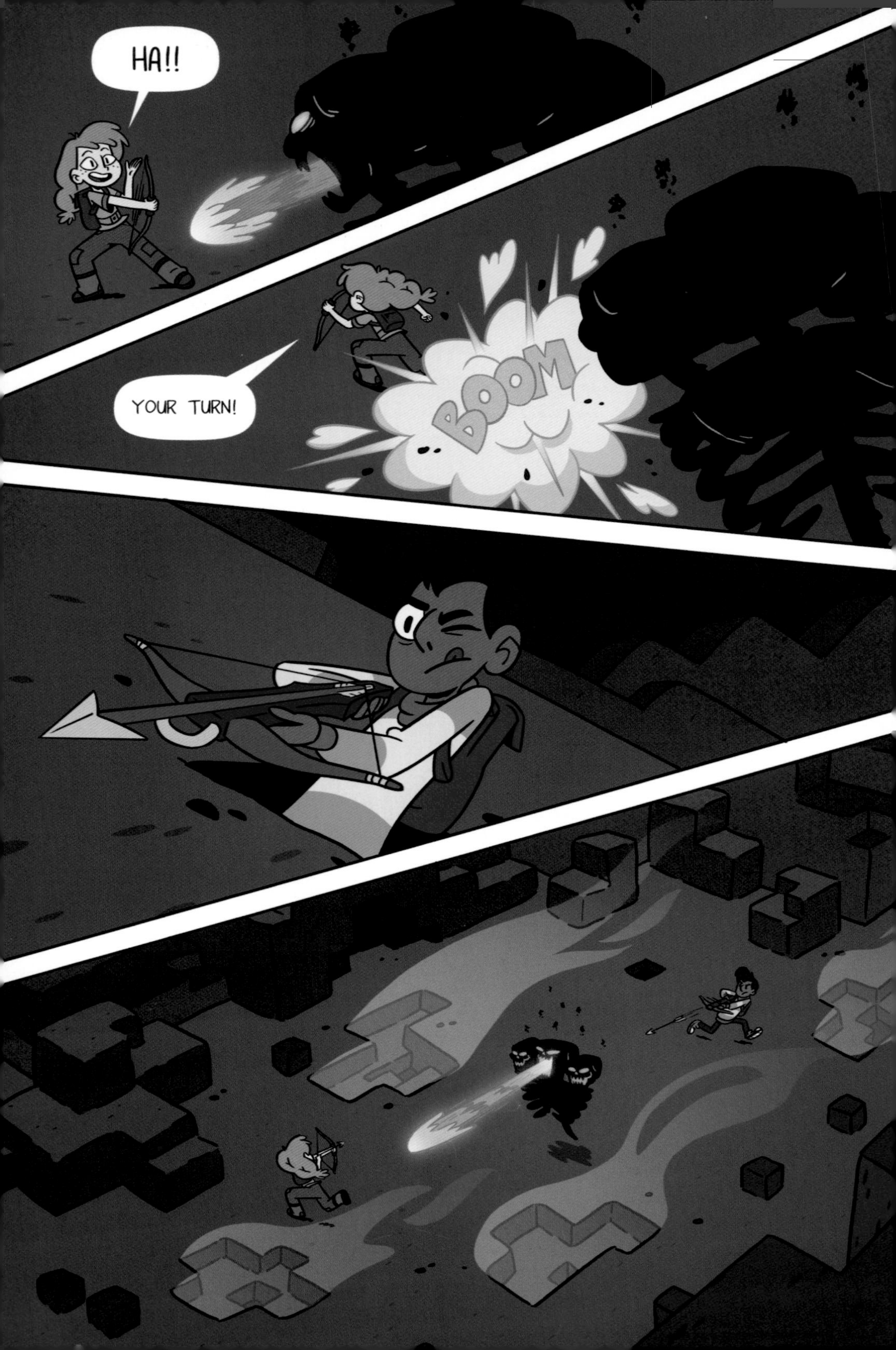
HA!!
YOUR TURN!
BOOM

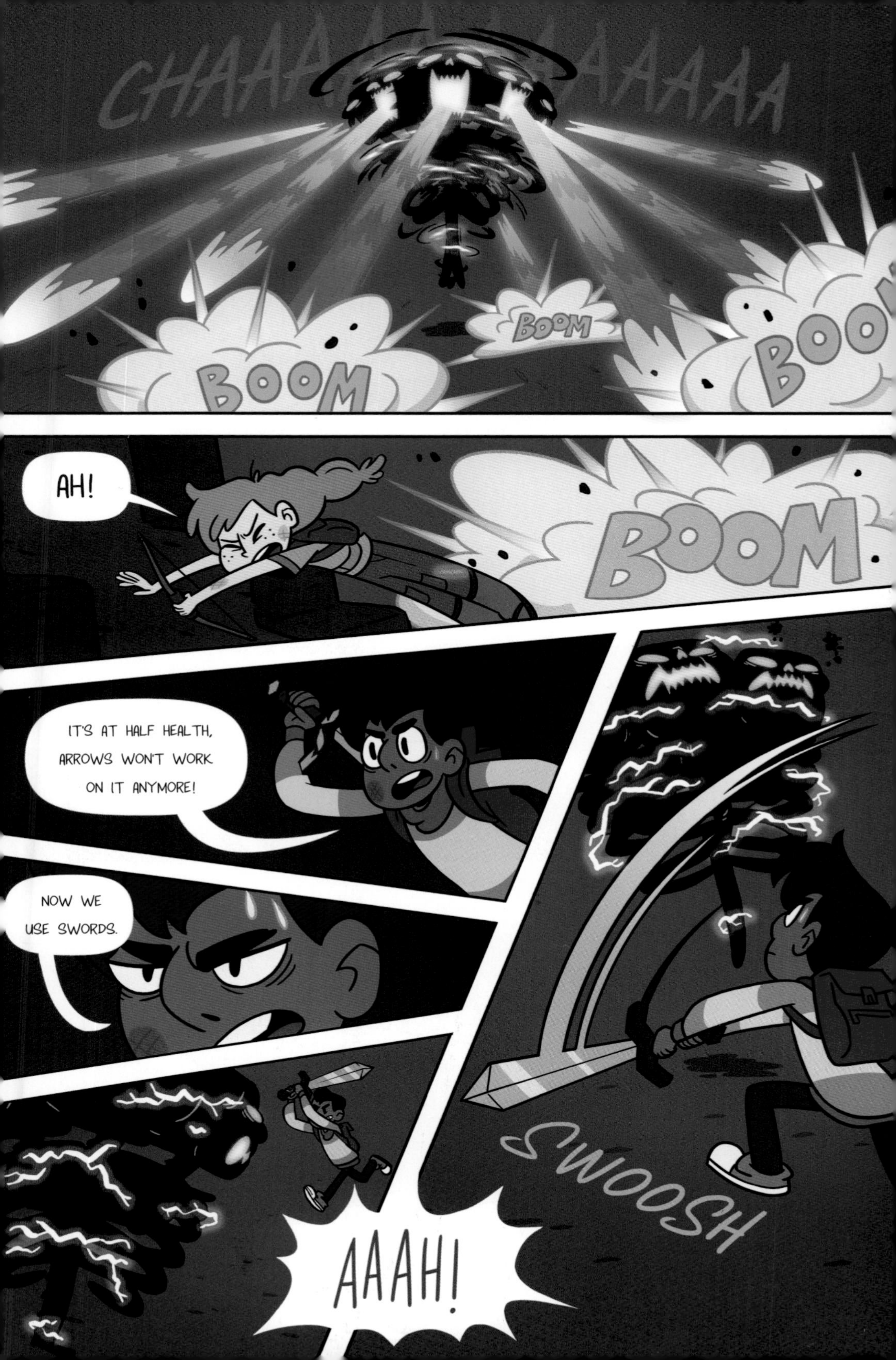
CHAAAAAAAAAAAA
BOOM
BOOM
BOOM
AH!
BOOM
IT'S AT HALF HEALTH, ARROWS WON'T WORK ON IT ANYMORE!
NOW WE USE SWORDS.
SWOOSH
AAAH!

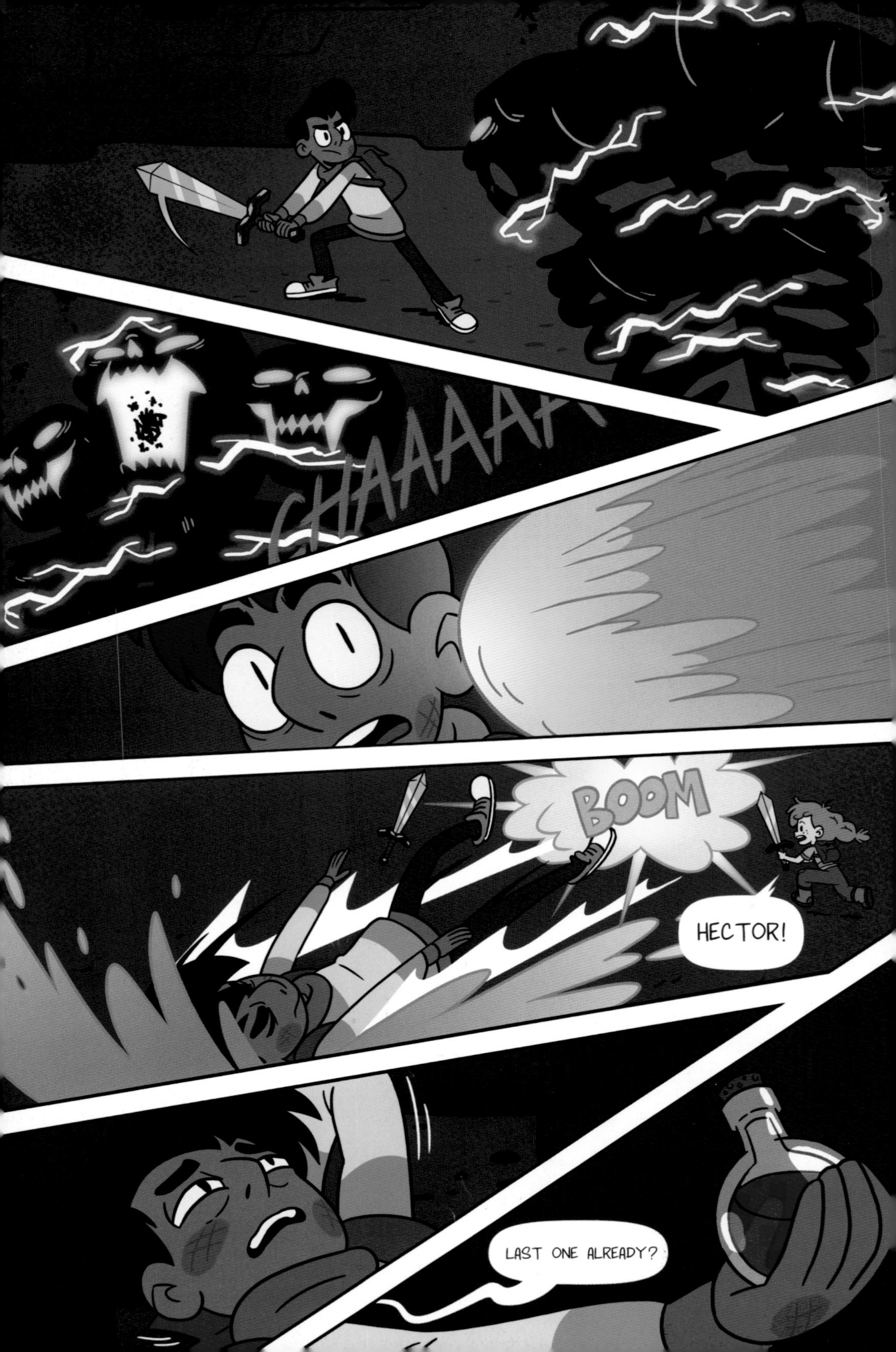
CHAAAAA
BOOM
HECTOR!
LAST ONE ALREADY?

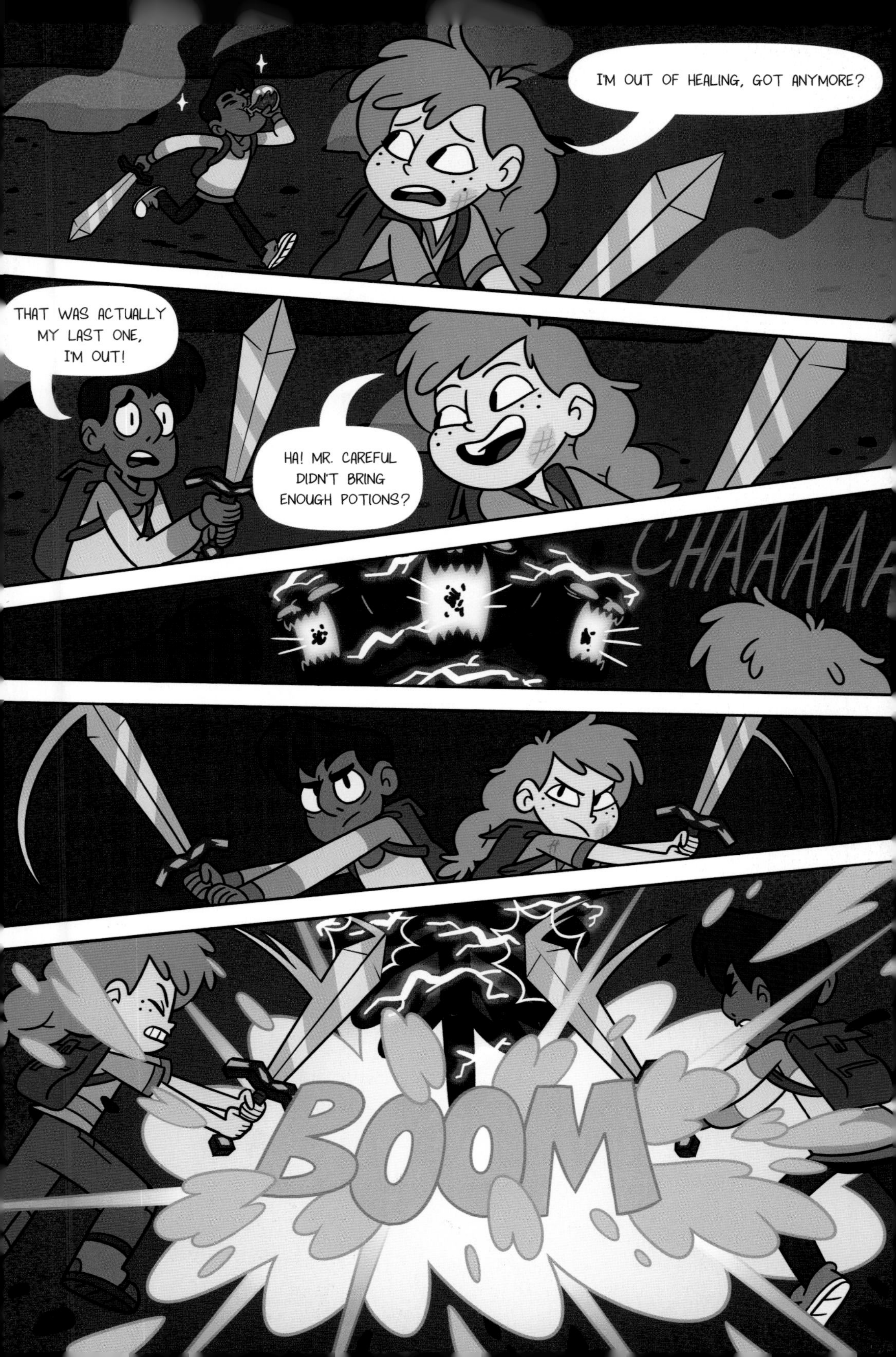
I'M OUT OF HEALING, GOT ANYMORE?
THAT WAS ACTUALLY MY LAST ONE, I'M OUT!
HA! MR. CAREFUL DIDN'T BRING ENOUGH POTIONS?
CHAAAAA
BOOM

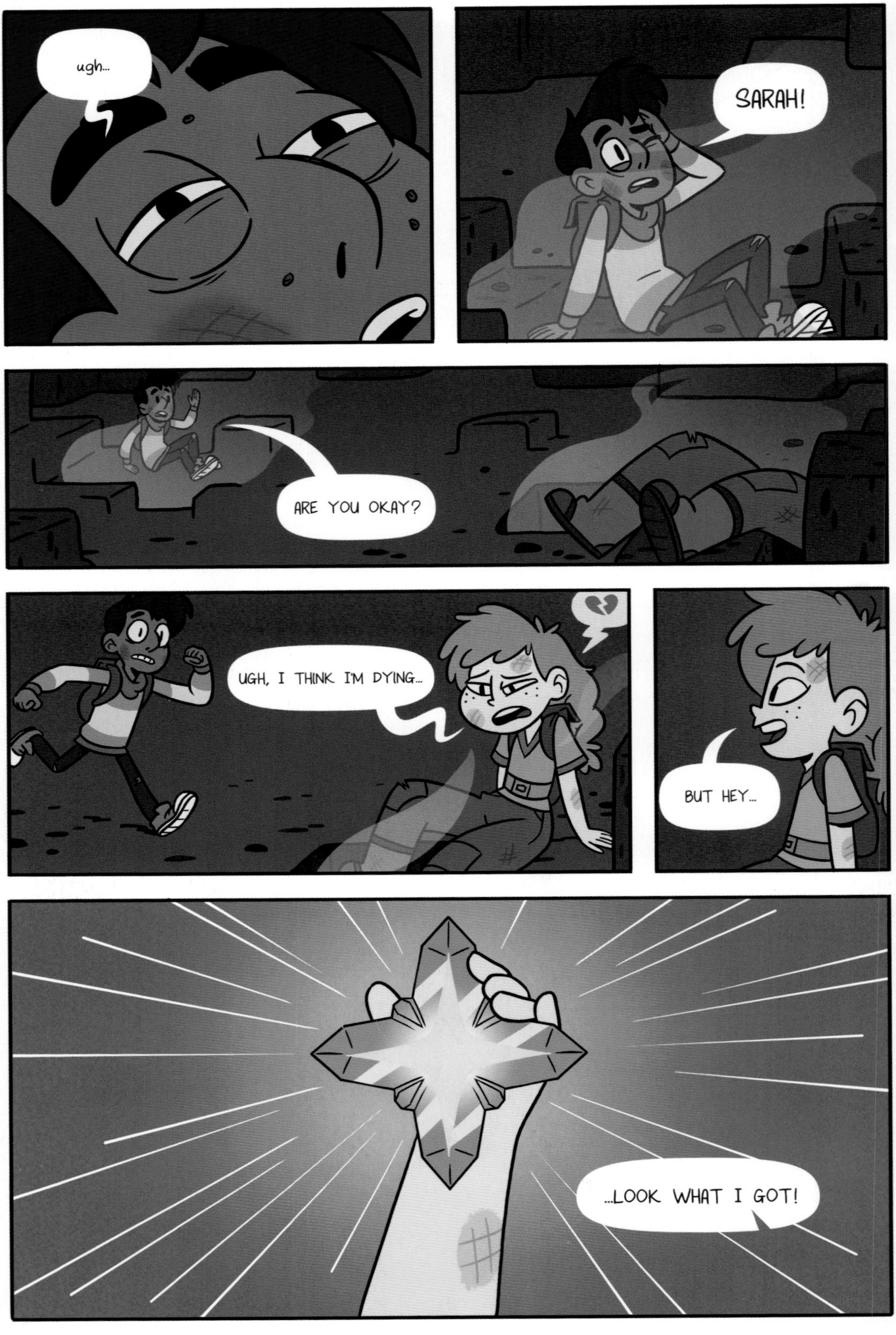
ugh...
SARAH!
ARE YOU OKAY?
UGH, I THINK I'M DYING...
BUT HEY...
...LOOK WHAT I GOT!

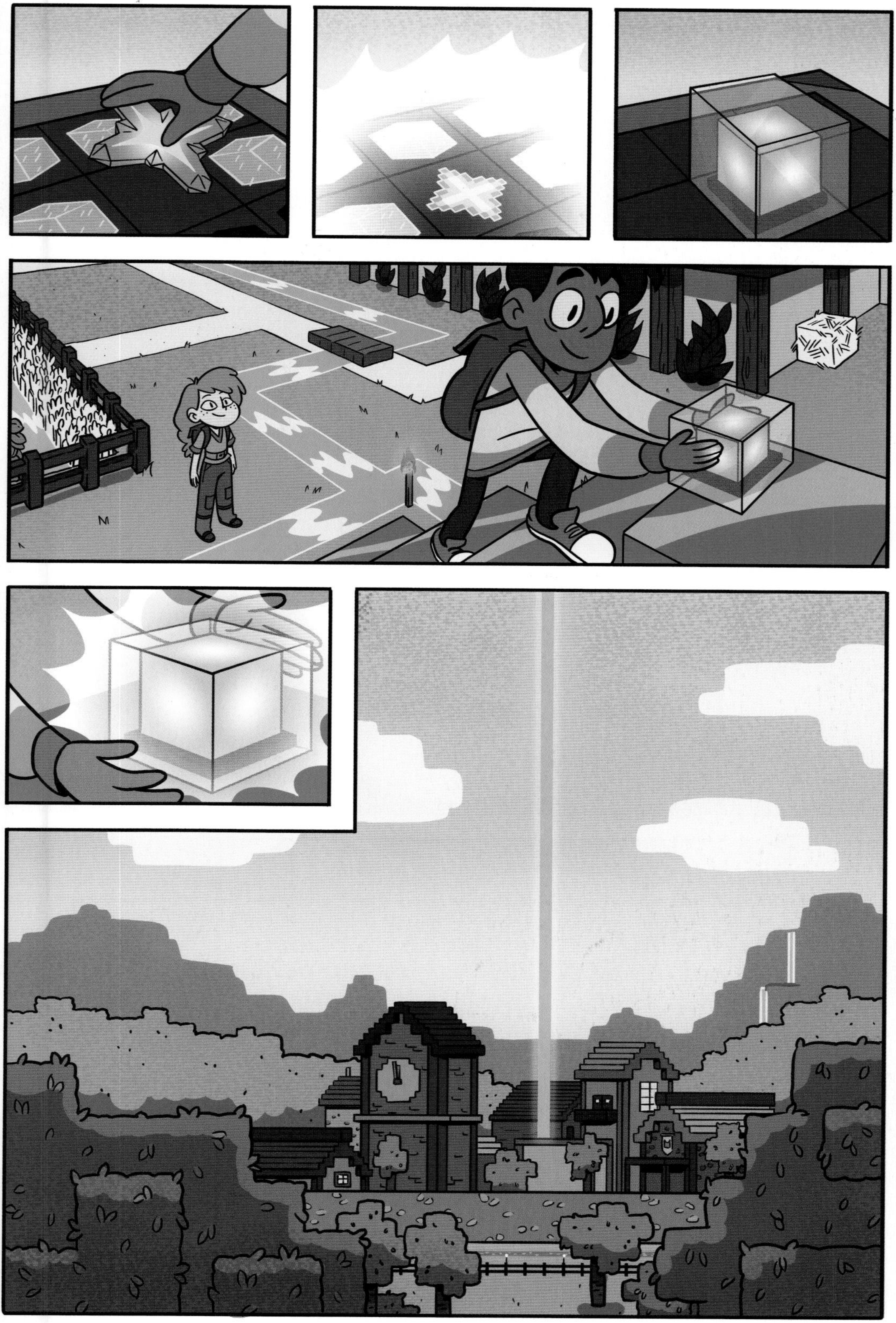

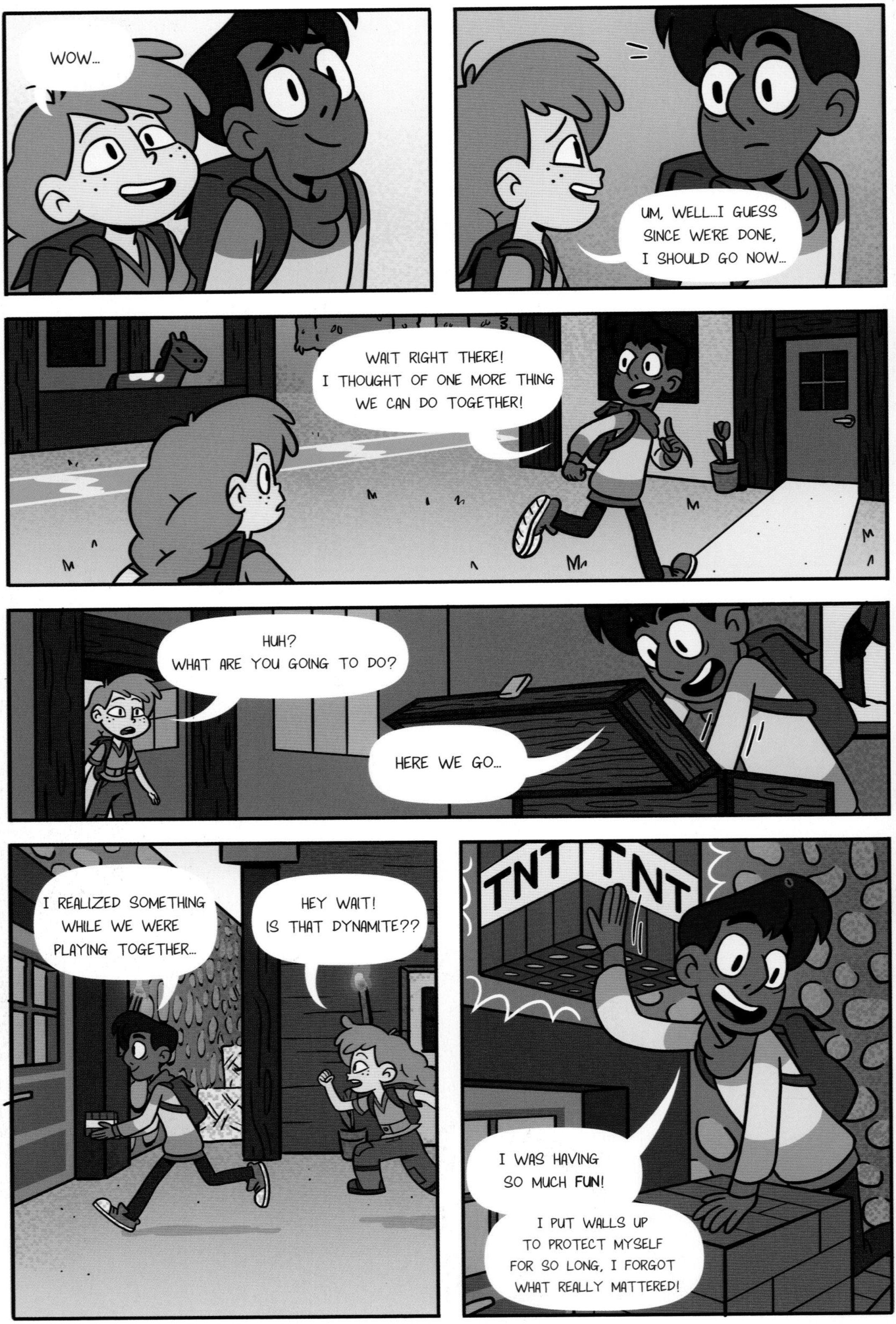
WOW...
UM, WELL...I GUESS SINCE WE'RE DONE, I SHOULD GO NOW...
WAIT RIGHT THERE! I THOUGHT OF ONE MORE THING WE CAN DO TOGETHER!
HUH? WHAT ARE YOU GOING TO DO?
HERE WE GO...
I REALIZED SOMETHING WHILE WE WERE PLAYING TOGETHER...
HEY WAIT! IS THAT DYNAMITE??
TNT TNT
I WAS HAVING SO MUCH FUN!
I PUT WALLS UP TO PROTECT MYSELF FOR SO LONG, I FORGOT WHAT REALLY MATTERED!

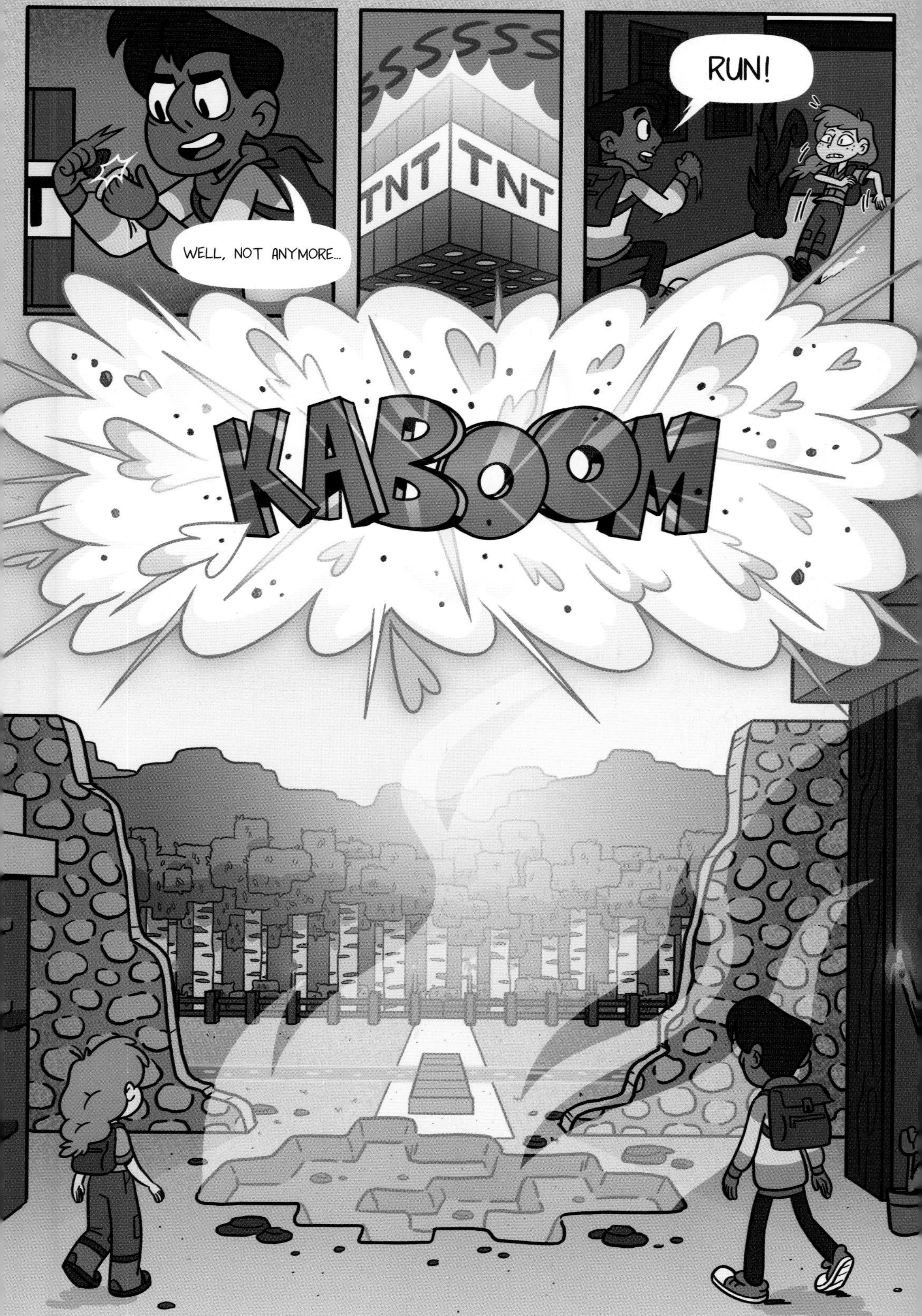
WELL, NOT ANYMORE...
SSSSSSS
TNT TNT
RUN!
KABOOM

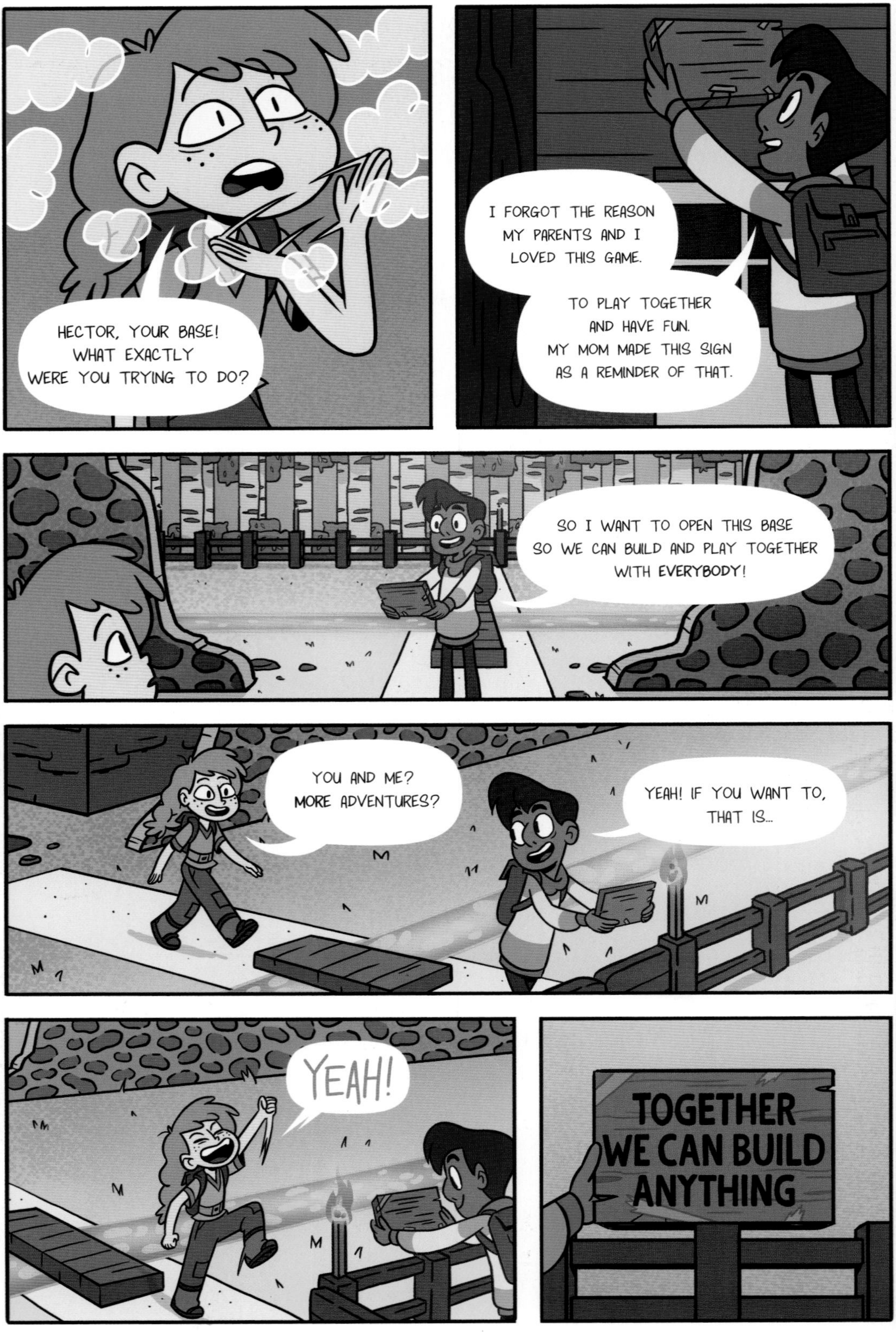
HECTOR, YOUR BASE! WHAT EXACTLY WERE YOU TRYING TO DO?
I FORGOT THE REASON MY PARENTS AND I LOVED THIS GAME.
TO PLAY TOGETHER AND HAVE FUN. MY MOM MADE THIS SIGN AS A REMINDER OF THAT.
SO I WANT TO OPEN THIS BASE SO WE CAN BUILD AND PLAY TOGETHER WITH EVERYBODY!
YOU AND ME? MORE ADVENTURES?
YEAH! IF YOU WANT TO, THAT IS...
YEAH!
TOGETHER WE CAN BUILD ANYTHING

MINECRAFT™ OPEN WORLD

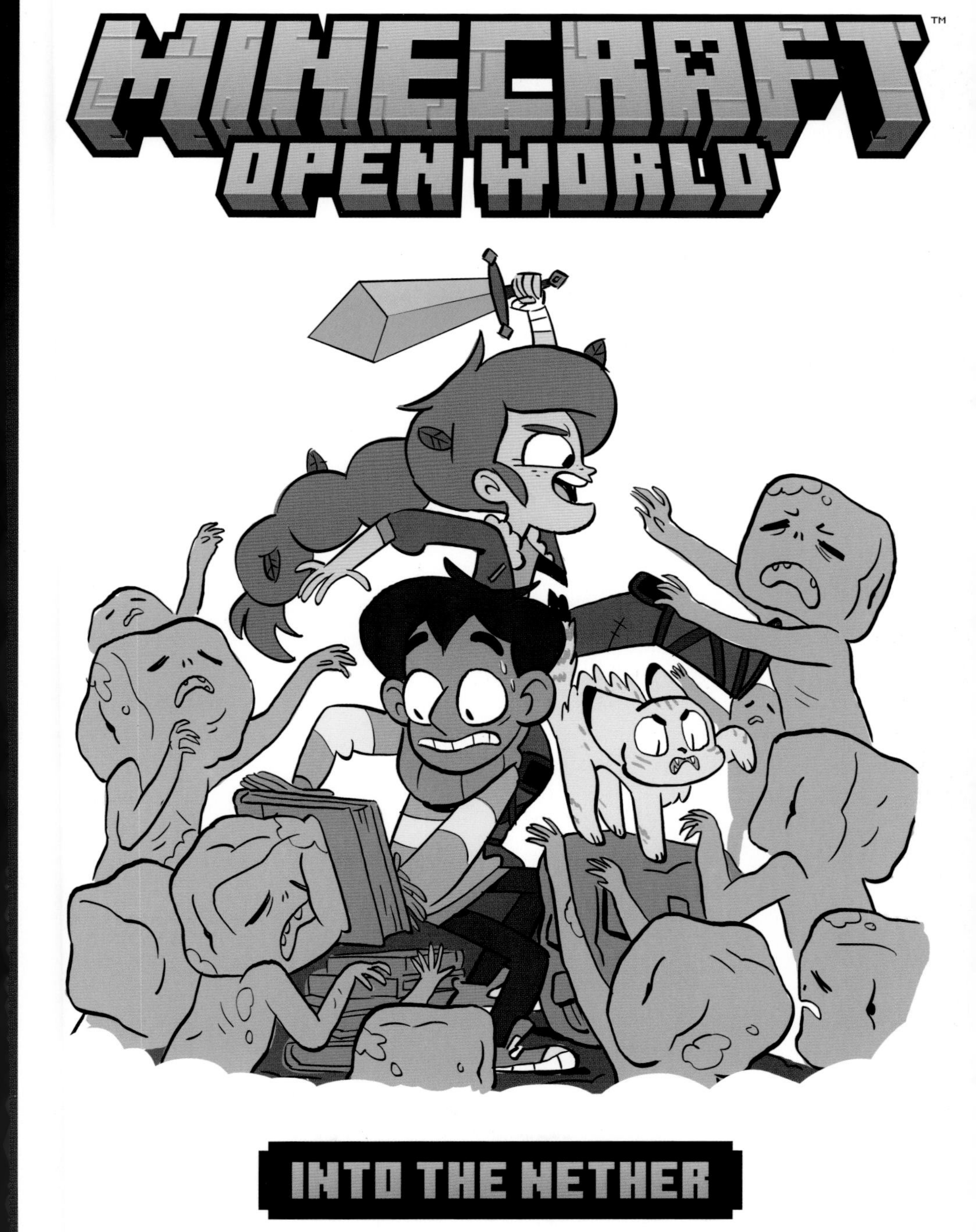

INTO THE NETHER

CONCEPT ART BY

STEPHANIE RAMIREZ

CONCEPT ART

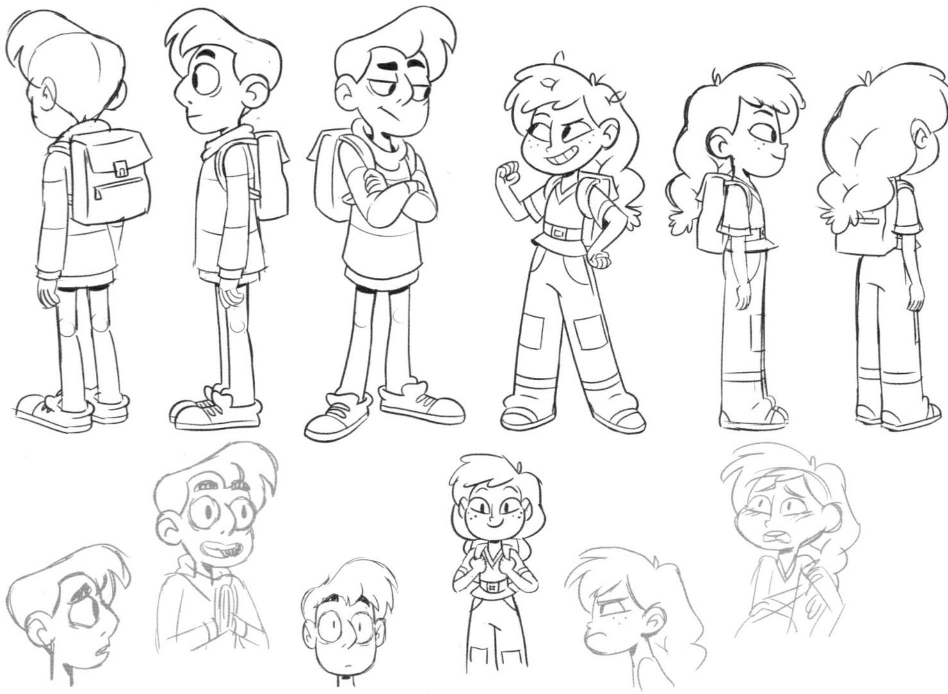

Initial character design sketches

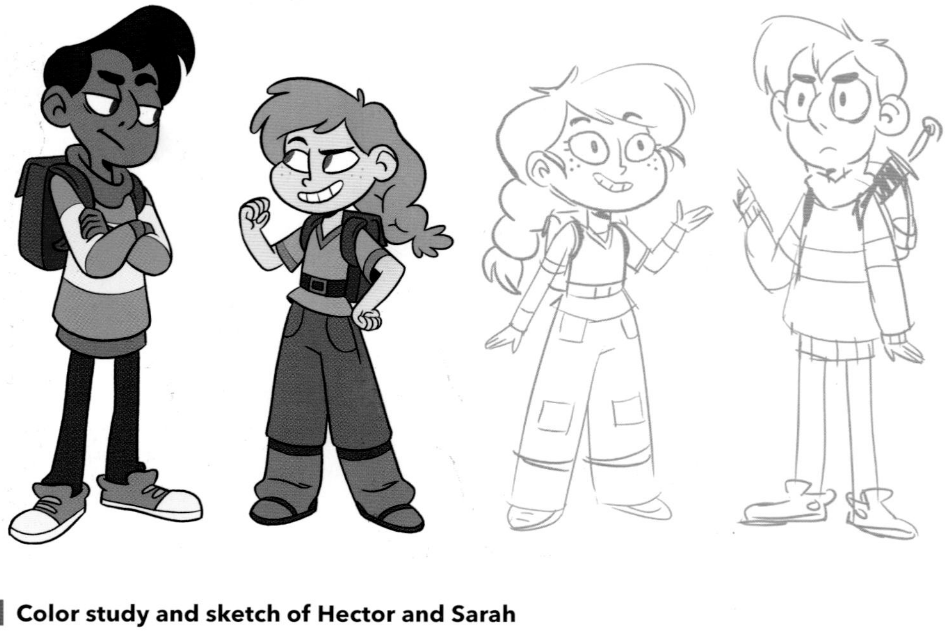

Color study and sketch of Hector and Sarah

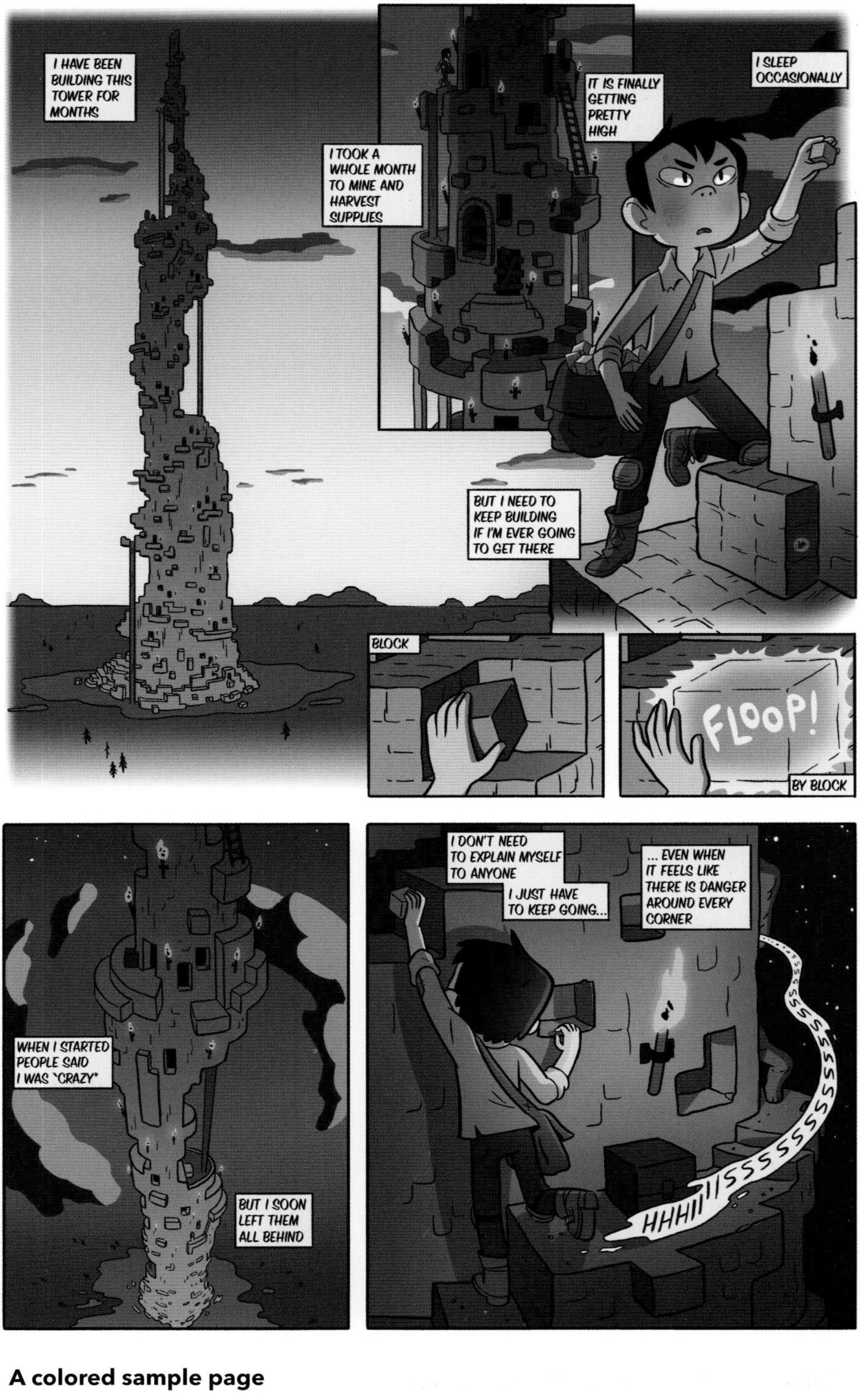
I HAVE BEEN BUILDING THIS TOWER FOR MONTHS
I TOOK A WHOLE MONTH TO MINE AND HARVEST SUPPLIES
IT IS FINALLY GETTING PRETTY HIGH
I SLEEP OCCASIONALLY
BUT I NEED TO KEEP BUILDING IF I'M EVER GOING TO GET THERE
BLOCK
FLOOP!
BY BLOCK
WHEN I STARTED PEOPLE SAID I WAS "CRAZY"
BUT I SOON LEFT THEM ALL BEHIND
I DON'T NEED TO EXPLAIN MYSELF TO ANYONE
I JUST HAVE TO KEEP GOING...
... EVEN WHEN IT FEELS LIKE THERE IS DANGER AROUND EVERY CORNER
HHHH!!SSSSSSSSSSSSSSSSSSSSS

A colored sample page

COVER ART PROCESS

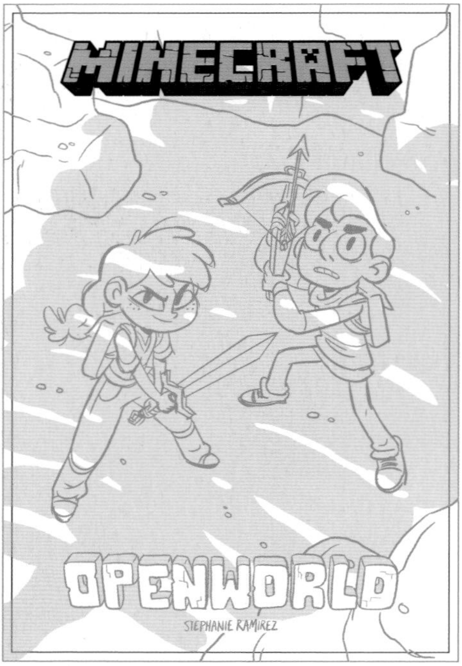
MINECRAFT
OPENWORLD
STEPHANIE RAMIREZ

Cover sketch option 1

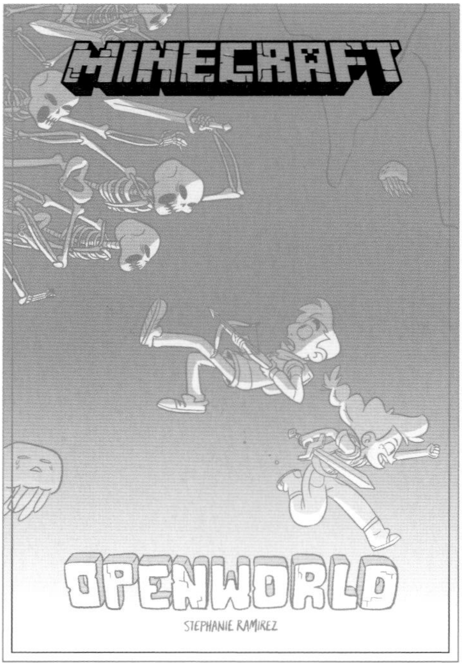
MINECRAFT
OPENWORLD
STEPHANIE RAMIREZ

Cover sketch option 2

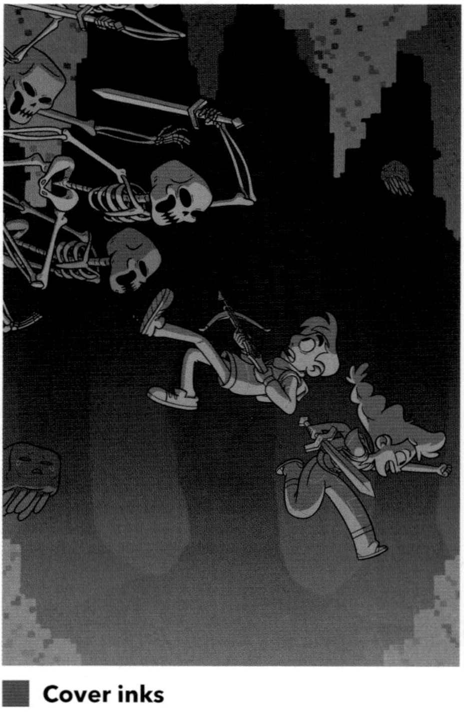

Cover inks

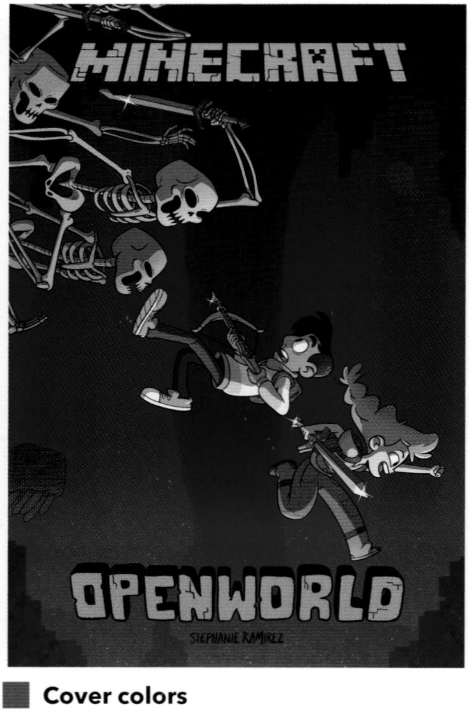
MINECRAFT
OPENWORLD
STEPHANIE RAMIREZ

Cover colors

FINAL COVER ART

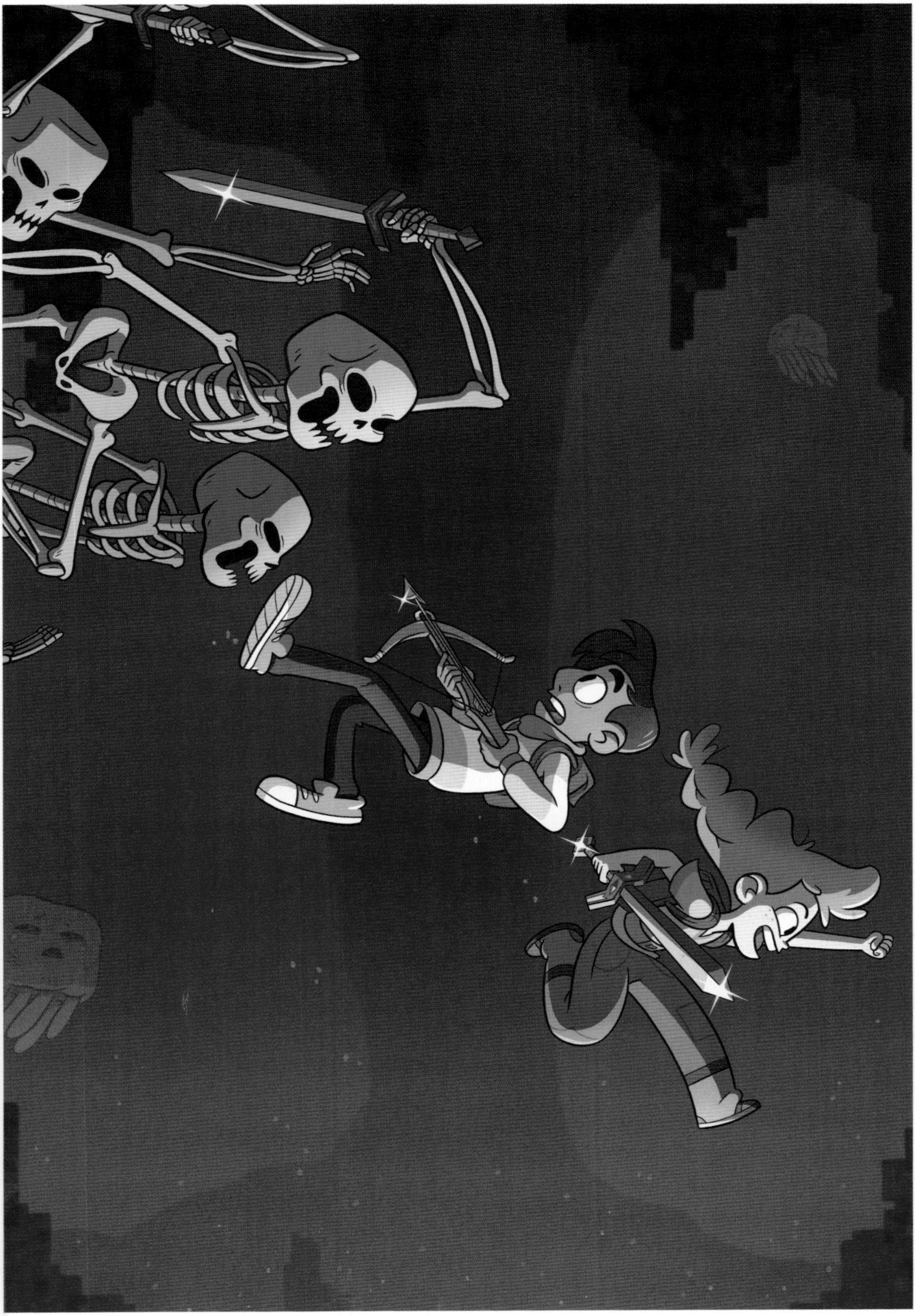

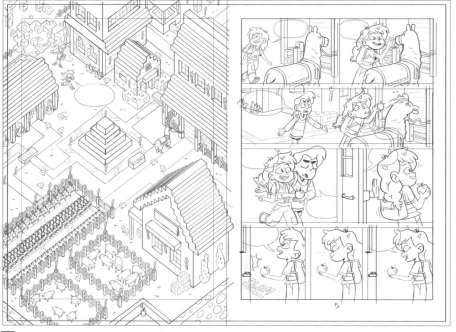

Pencils for pages 04 and 05

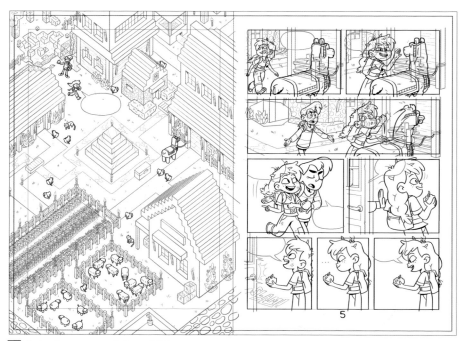

Inks for pages 04 and 05

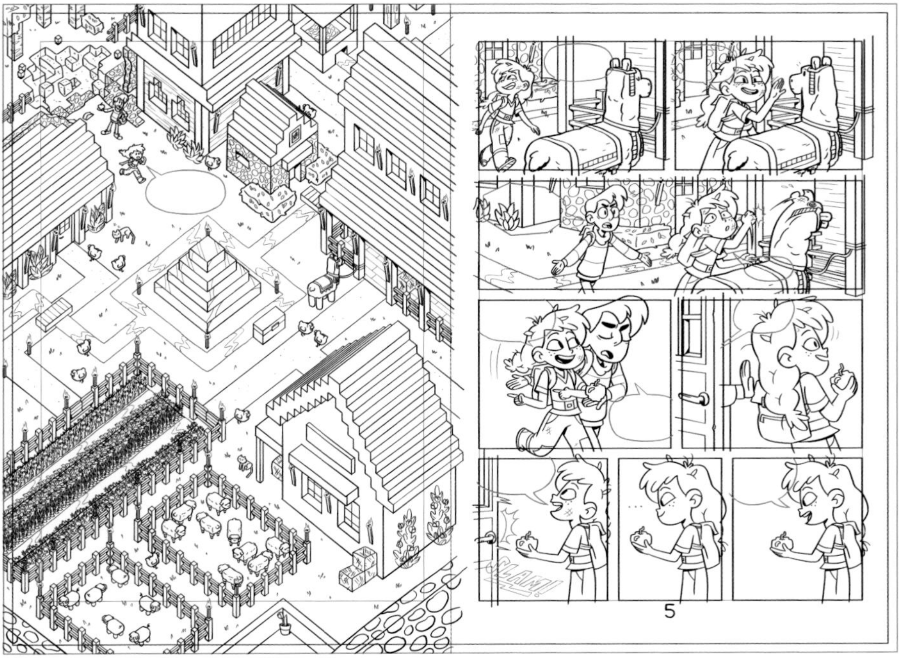
CLAM!
5

Revised inks for pages 04 and 05

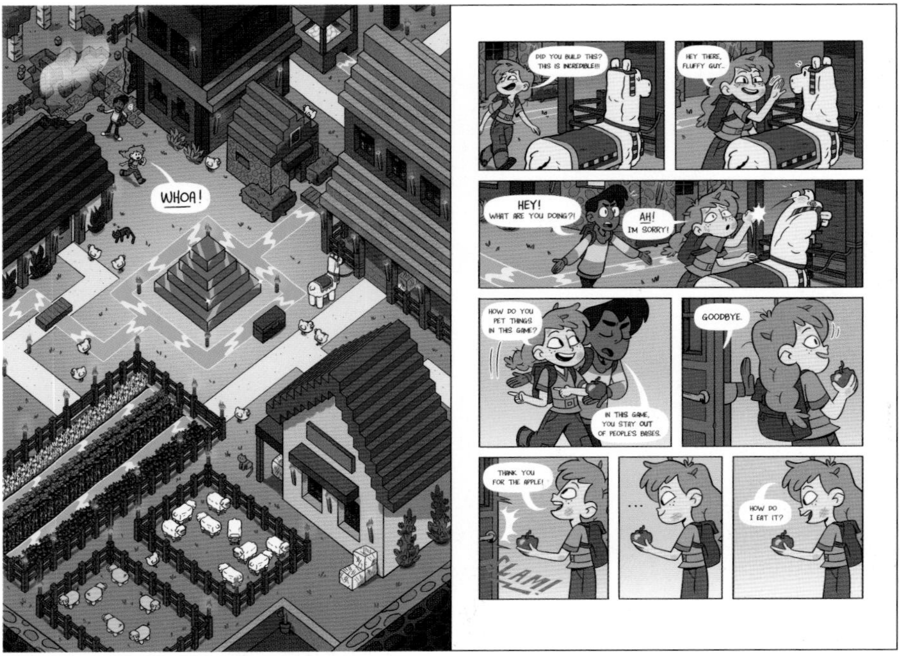
WHOA!
DID YOU BUILD THIS? THIS IS INCREDIBLE!!!
HEY THERE, FLUFFY GUY...
HEY! WHAT ARE YOU DOING?!
AH! I'M SORRY!
HOW DO YOU PET THINGS IN THIS GAME?
IN THIS GAME, YOU STAY OUT OF PEOPLE'S BASES.
GOODBYE.
THANK YOU FOR THE APPLE!
SLAM!
...
HOW DO I EAT IT?

Completed art for Pages 04 and 05

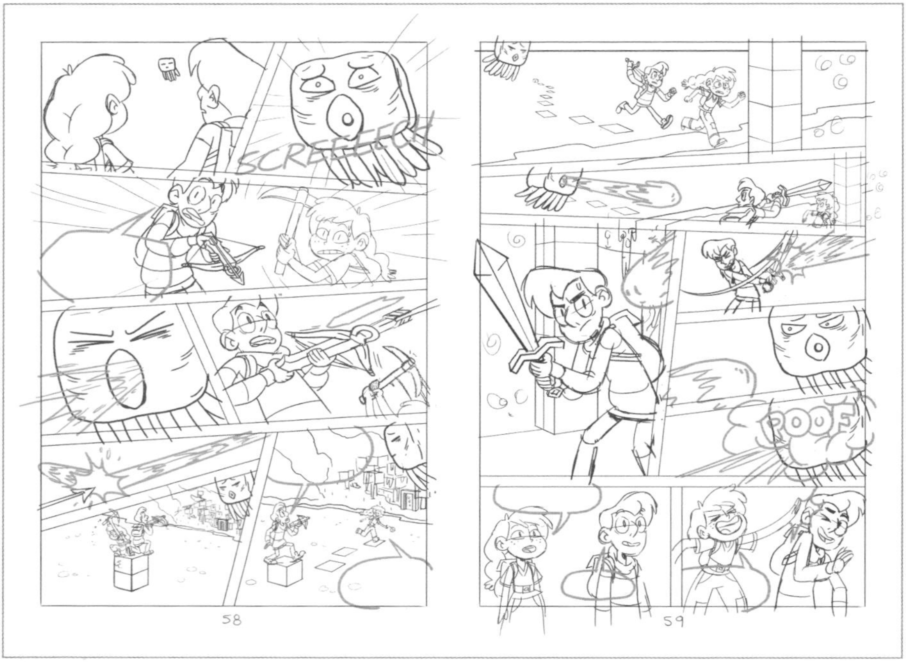
SCREEEECH
POOF
58
59

Pencils for pages 58 and 59

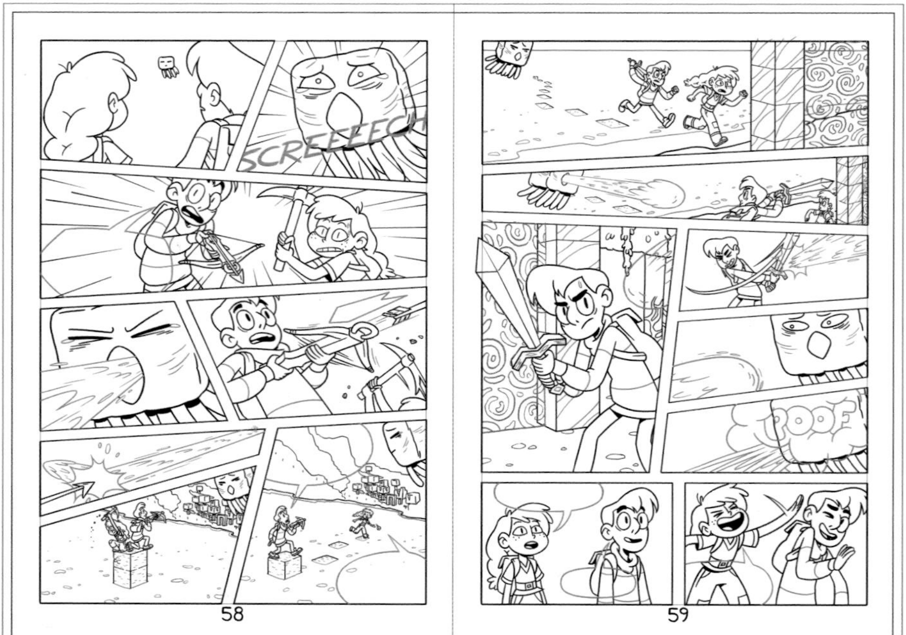
SCREEEECH
POOF
58
59

Inks for pages 58 and 59

PAGE CREATION

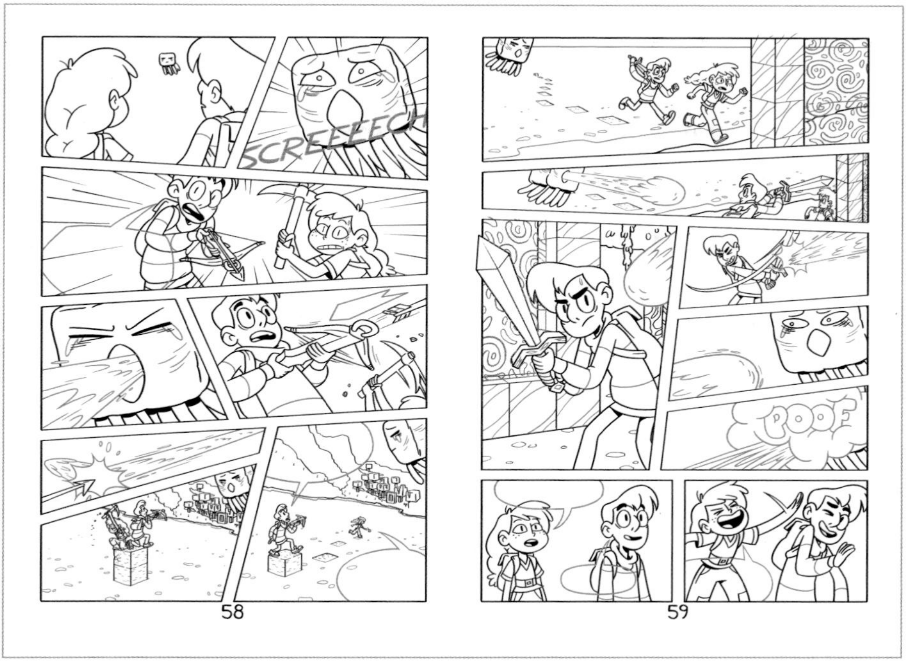
SCREEEECH
58
POOF
59

Revised inks for pages 58 and 59

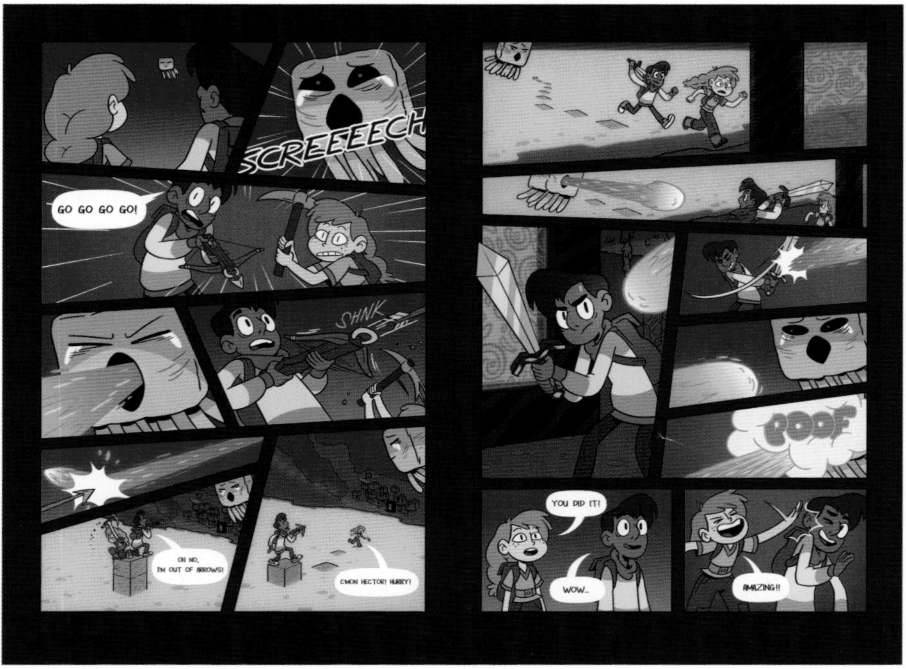
SCREEEECH
GO GO GO GO!
SHNK
OH NO, I'M OUT OF ARROWS!
C'MON HECTOR! HURRY!
POOF
YOU DID IT!
WOW...
AMAZING!!

Completed art for Pages 58 and 59

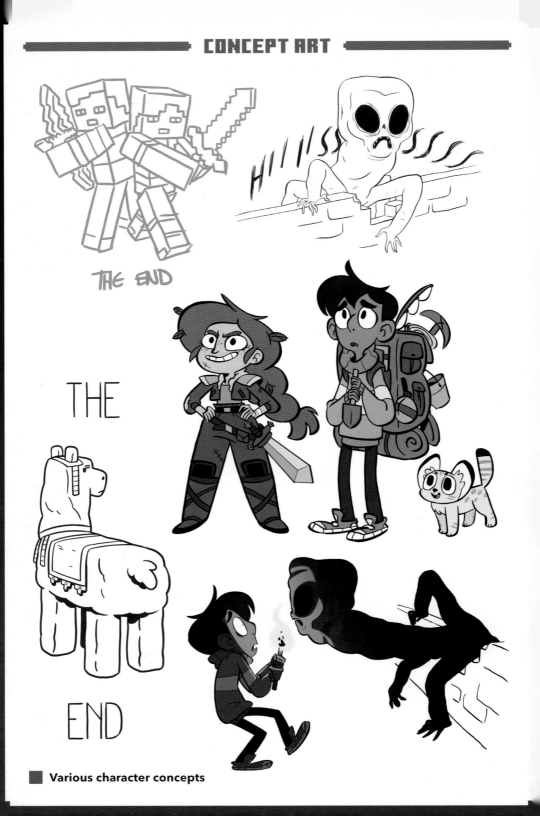

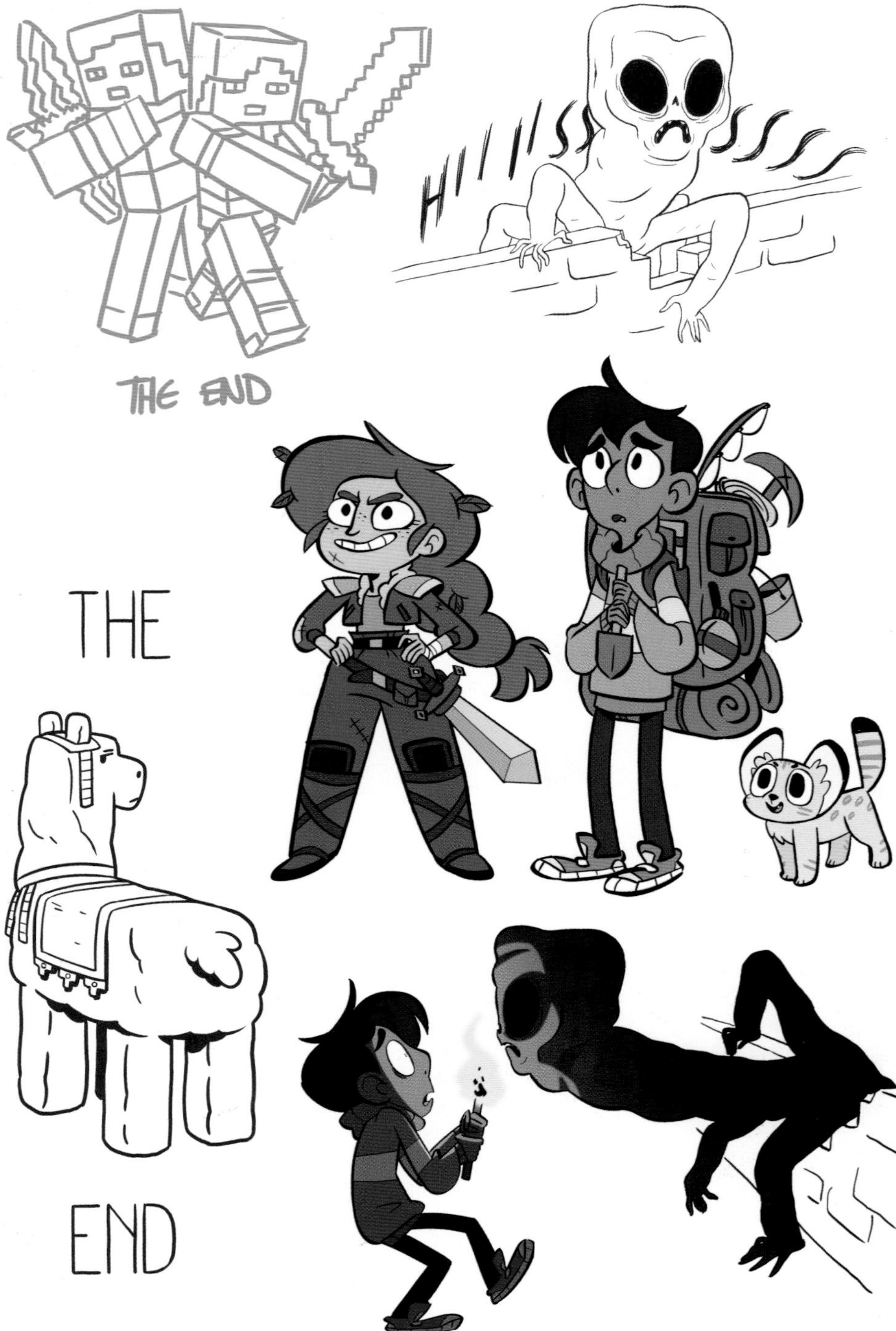
THE END
THE
END

Various character concepts